# STILL OF
# THE NIGHT

Other books by Cynthia Danielewski:

*Night Fire*
*Night Moves*
*Realm of Darkness*
*Dead of Night*
*After Dark*
*Edge of Night*

# STILL OF
# THE NIGHT

•

# Cynthia Danielewski

*AVALON BOOKS*
NEW YORK

Published by Thomas Bouregy & Co., Inc.
160 Madison Avenue, New York, NY 10016

Library of Congress Cataloging-in-Publication Data

Danielewski, Cynthia.
    Still of the night / Cynthia Danielewski.
        p.    cm.
    ISBN 978-0-8034-9918-8 (acid-free paper)
    1. Long Island (N.Y.)—Fiction.    I. Title.

PS3604.A528S75 2008
813'.6—dc22                                    2008017343

PRINTED IN THE UNITED STATES OF AMERICA
ON ACID-FREE PAPER
BY HADDON CRAFTSMEN, BLOOMSBURG, PENNSYLVANIA

## Chapter One

New York Police Detective Jack Reeves stepped out onto the glistening deck of the luxury yacht *Aphrodite* that had been rented for the night in honor of police Captain Ed Stall's fiftieth birthday. The USCG-certified vessel was one hundred and twenty-four feet of gleaming white fiberglass with large panoramic windows, and boasted three levels of entertainment space for guests to enjoy. Ed's family had gone all out to ensure that the man's birthday would be celebrated in style, and Jack had to admit that they had done a wonderful job in making the occasion memorable. In addition to the luxurious surroundings, the catered buffet dinner had been exceptionally good, and the band had many of the couples on the floor dancing. Overall, the night was going extremely well.

Walking over to the railing that was draped with miniature white lights, Jack looked out over the dark Long Island Sound. The night air was warm with a slight summer breeze, and a peaceful tranquility whispered over the water as the yacht floated gently from where they had dropped anchor. As he looked into the dark expanse, he wondered briefly what his small son John was doing. Tonight was one of the rare occasions that Jack and his wife Ashley had left him with a babysitter, and Jack missed spending time with him. Evenings spent with just his wife and his son were what he looked forward to the most.

"Escaping?" a soft feminine voice asked, breaking into his reverie.

Jack turned, his facial expression softening as he saw Ashley. "Hi." He beckoned her closer, his gaze following her as she made her way over to him. He couldn't help but think how beautiful she looked in the moonlit night. The strapless white evening gown that she purchased specifically for Ed's party highlighted her summer tan, and brought attention to the blond highlights in her hair and the rich brown color of her eyes.

Ashley walked over, her hand reaching up to brush gently through the short strands of Jack's black hair that wafted about in the soft breeze. Her fingers skimmed over the long scar from his temple to his mouth, a souvenir from his very first case as a homicide detective, well over a decade ago. "Everything okay?"

Jack grimaced wryly. "Yeah. I just wanted to get some air. It's pretty crowded in there." He motioned to the dining salon that was filled almost to capacity with jovial guests.

Ashley smiled in understanding, knowing that her husband usually tried to avoid social settings such as this. Jack preferred quiet evenings spent at home. He had never been one for parties. "It will be over soon enough."

"I know," he said, enfolding her in his embrace. "Enjoying yourself?"

"I always enjoy myself when I'm with you."

"The feeling's mutual," he assured her, kissing her tenderly.

Ashley smiled and settled contentedly in his arms, her gaze wandering to the festivities inside. "Ryan and Jane seem to be enjoying the dance floor," she said, making a reference to Jack's police partner Ryan Parks and his date, Jane Ramsey.

Jack gave a slight laugh and looked through the open doorway to where the twosome could be seen slow dancing. There was no doubt that the two of them had eyes for only each other. "Yeah, I noticed that," he replied dryly, thinking that they made an unlikely pair. Though Ryan was one of the best cops Jack knew, his unconventional physical appearance was often at odds with his conservative work ethics.

Already well into his fifties, Ryan had a tendency to wear his gray-streaked brown hair long and clubbed in the back, conveying the image of a laid-back hippy. It was a style that he had cultivated years ago when he worked undercover in the narcotics division, long before he transferred to homicide, and one that he seemed comfortable presenting to the outside world. By contrast, Jane was always impeccably groomed. Jack didn't think that he had ever seen the petite, auburn-haired woman with a hair out of place, or without manicured hands.

"They make a nice couple," Ashley murmured, turning her attention away from the party inside. Shifting in her husband's arms so that she could look out over the water, she rested back against his chest. "What were you thinking about a little while ago? You looked preoccupied."

"I was wondering if John was okay."

Ashley smiled. Jack doted on their son. Nobody would ever dispute that. "He's with my aunt. He's fine."

"I'm sure he is. But I still miss him."

"Me too," she acknowledged softly, her hand reaching for his and squeezing it slightly in empathy. After a long pause of silence, she said, "The night's beautiful."

Jack placed a light kiss against her temple. "So are you."

Ashley was about to teasingly respond when she

felt his arms tense. "What's the matter?" she asked, turning to look at him. She noticed he was focused on the water. She turned back around to see what had captured his attention but the only thing she saw was a clump of seaweed floating in the gentle surf.

"I'm not sure," Jack said, releasing Ashley from his arms and moving closer to the railing. "I thought I saw something."

"The seaweed?"

"No. Something else that caught the reflection of the moonlight." He took a few steps back and glanced around until he caught sight of an extended pole resting in a corner of an alcove. Reaching for it, he turned back to the railing and gently began prodding the mass of vegetation.

"Jack?" Ashley did not see anything that should have caused his reaction.

"There's something there," Jack stated, watching as the seaweed began to break apart.

Ashley finally caught sight of the pale object that Jack was trying to uncover. Curious about what it was, she watched as he stretched out over the yacht to push away the remaining seaweed with the pole. The moment he did, she jerked back. She stared in horror as the dead body of a woman broke the surface.

## Chapter Two

Ashley's hand flew to her mouth. "Jack!"

"Go inside and get Ryan and Ed," Jack ordered grimly, his full attention on the woman whose body floated lifeless in Long Island Sound. Quickly shrugging out of his suit jacket, he carelessly tossed the garment onto the deck before stepping onto the fixed boarding ladder attached to the side of the yacht. Lowering himself on the rungs, he grabbed the handrail tightly as he stretched out to grab the woman, unmindful of the water that was lapping against his pants and shoes.

Jack had just managed to grab onto her clothing when Ryan Parks and Ed Stall swiftly made their way to the side of the railing. They were followed by several other police personnel as well as some of the

6

yacht's crew that had made it past the officer Ed assigned to keep anybody who wasn't police off the deck. Almost simultaneously, the entire area surrounding the yacht was illuminated as the sidelights of the vessel were turned on.

"Hold on!" Ryan called to Jack, stepping over the railing so that he could help. Anchoring himself to the outer edge of the deck, he crouched down and helped Jack pull the woman's body toward the ship, getting her in position to lift from the water.

Jack cast a quick glance at Ryan. "On the count of three. One, two, three . . ."

Ryan grunted as they managed to heave the dead weight from the water and pass her to Ed and another officer waiting to lift her over the railing.

"Of all things . . ." Ed muttered harshly once he had the body on board. His pale blue eyes slashed to Jack. "Ashley said that you were the one who noticed the woman. Did you see anything that would explain what happened?"

Jack made his way back over the railing. "No. If it weren't for the moonlight reflecting off the water, I probably wouldn't have noticed anything. She was pretty entangled in the seaweed."

"Meaning, she's been floating a while," Ryan said as he too made his way back over the rail.

"It looks that way," Jack stated before turning to Ed. "We'll need to keep the crowd controlled so that no evidence is compromised."

Ed nodded and turned to one of the other detectives, Paul Murphy. "Murphy, get everybody back inside. We'll bring out additional personnel as they're needed."

Murphy nodded and started ushering the people back inside. "I'll take care of it."

"This is my ship and I'd like to help. Tell me what I can do," a deep voice directed from somewhere off to the side.

Jack turned, instantly recognizing the man that spoke. He was the yacht's captain, Jim McCall. Ed had introduced them before they left dock. "We need something to lay her on. Do you have anything we can use?" he asked, not surprised that the ship's captain wanted to stay and help. The man had struck Jack as someone with high principles and ideals. Retired from the Navy, McCall still maintained the persona with his closely cropped gray hair and trim stocky frame, as well as with his mannerisms. The formality that he and his crew displayed was an indication that he had a deep sense of propriety and maintained a strong level of control.

McCall nodded and quickly left the area, returning moments later with a heavy waterproof tarp. "It's not much, but it's the best I can do," he said, laying the tarp out on the deck.

"It's fine," Jack assured him, knowing that the important thing was to preserve as much physical evidence as possible. Glancing at Ryan and Ed, Jack said, "Let's move her."

The moment they lifted the woman onto the tarp, Jack sat back on his heels, his eyes assessing the condition of her body. The maceration of her skin caused by the absorption of water was minimal, it could only be seen in the fingertips. Taking into account the relative warmth of the water, Jack estimated that the woman hadn't been submerged for long. "She's been in the water for at least a couple of hours."

Ed grunted and raked a hand through his thick thatch of gray hair. He took a moment to study the woman. The slightly bluish cast to her skin contrasted sharply with her pale blond hair, but it was the way she was dressed that gained his full attention. She was wearing shorts, a T-shirt, and running shoes. "One thing is obvious. This wasn't some accidental drowning caused by a summer night's swim."

"No, it's not. Look at her wrists and ankles," Jack said, studying the red indentations noticeable on her skin.

Ryan frowned at Jack's words and looked closer at the body. Crouching down, he took a look at the abrasions. "Someone tied her up."

"Either that or they tried to weigh her down," Jack stated.

Ed frowned and turned to McCall. "We need to

start heading back to dock, but before we do I'd like to mark the spot where the body was found. Do you have a floating marker we could use? It'll make it easier for the underwater search and recovery unit's divers to search the area. I'll also need our exact co-ordinates. We'll need to see if there's any evidence in the water associated with this woman's death."

McCall nodded and quickly went to retrieve a diver's flag. After placing it in the water, he said, "I'll get you the coordinates."

"Thanks. We'd also like to start questioning your employees. There's a possibility that one of the people onboard the ship saw or heard something that might help us find whoever was responsible for killing this woman."

"My crew will offer their full cooperation."

Jack asked, "How many employees do you have?"

"About twenty. Fifteen are present on the ship tonight. That's how many people I estimated would be needed to take care of the crowd."

"We'll need a list of the names, addresses, and phone numbers of all the people in your employ," Jack told him.

"Of course. Did you want just the ones that worked tonight?"

"I'd like everybody's," Jack said, knowing that it might prove useful during the investigation.

McCall nodded. "I can give it to you tonight. I keep a copy onboard."

"We'd appreciate that."

"It's not a problem."

"How far are we from the port?" Ryan asked, knowing that they had been anchored for the last few hours.

"Several miles, but it won't take us long to get back," McCall replied.

Ed's gaze encompassed Jack and Ryan. "I'll arrange for our own people to meet us there. I'll also give the instruction for them to start questioning any people that are in the area. Maybe someone saw the woman earlier, or saw something suspicious."

"I'll show you where the radio is and get you the coordinates," McCall said, turning to lead the way.

"I'll be back as soon as I cover everything on my end," Ed promised Jack and Ryan.

Jack reached for an end of the tarp to cover the woman before standing and walking over the railing to look out over the expanse of water. As he did, he rolled up the damp sleeves of his shirt and loosened the knot on his tie.

"Do you see anything?" Ryan asked, grimacing at the wetness of his own suit jacket. He removed the garment and tossed it onto the deck to join Jack's. His eyes searched the water, looking for anything out of the ordinary, any physical evidence that might be floating.

"Nothing that would give any clues as to what happened to the victim."

"We're not that far off shore. Maybe her death occurred on the beach and her body was carried out by the current," Ryan suggested.

"I think it's more likely that someone deliberately tried to dispose of the body from a boat."

"Because of the marks on her wrists and ankles? It's possible she was tied up before she was killed. We won't know her exact cause of death until we get the autopsy report."

"Well, hopefully the coroner gives this case the priority it needs so that we'll have some answers soon."

Ryan silently agreed. Turning slightly, his eyes took in the disorder in the dining salon as the off-duty police officers tried to get organized. The shock on the faces of the crew and the guests was evident, and he knew that getting people to cooperate in an organized manner wasn't going to be an easy task. Everybody was on edge. "I'm going to go inside and see if they need any help setting up the interviews."

Jack nodded slightly. "Let me know if something surfaces."

"Count on it," Ryan replied.

Fifteen minutes later, Ed walked back to where Jack waited by the railing.

"Did you arrange everything?" Jack asked.

Ed pushed a ruthless hand through his hair. "Yeah. They'll meet us at the dock and I gave the order to dispatch a team over to the port. They should be arriving there shortly." After a moment he added, "Ryan and some of the other officers started interviewing people."

"I know. Are your guests included in the people being questioned?"

"Yeah. I'm not sure if anything will show there, but it's worth a shot. It's possible someone came out on deck and saw something."

"I'd like to go in and see how things are progressing. Will you stay with the body?"

"Not a problem."

"I'll be back soon."

As Jack entered the dining salon, he was immediately struck by the ominous tension in the air. What was once a party atmosphere only a short while ago had quickly transformed into a full-scaled police investigation. The officers had rearranged the room, pushing wood dining tables stripped of their white linens close together, and shifting the upholstered chairs to set up small conference areas. Lights that had been dimmed during the party's festivities now burned brightly, the harsh lighting doing little to hide the stress on people's faces. The somber heaviness that filled the air was almost tangible as people waited impatiently on the sidelines to speak with the officers that had been recruited to help with the interviewing process.

Jack's eyes searched the room, and he easily

recognized Ed's guests among the crowd. All of the people invited to celebrate Ed's birthday were dressed in semi-formal attire, while the employees of the yacht were all wearing a similar uniform of black pants, a white shirt, and a short black jacket. Jack was grateful for the distinction. He knew it would make it easier to keep track of everyone.

He saw Ryan sitting in a corner interviewing a tall, red-haired woman with vivid green eyes that Jack recognized as one of the wait staff. Jack made his way over to them.

Ryan looked up. "Jack, I'm glad you're here. I'd like you to meet Kate Walter."

He shook the woman's hand. "Detective Jack Reeves."

The woman looked back to Ryan with uncertainty, and Jack took a moment to study her. She was young, early twenties, and very nervous. He had noticed before he came over that she had repeatedly run her hand through her long tumble of curls, and he felt the same hand tremble when he shook it. He wondered if it was just the natural nervousness that people experienced when they spoke to the authorities, or something else. When she shifted uncomfortably in her chair, Jack's eyes met Ryan's.

"Ms. Walter and I were just starting to talk," Ryan said with an element in his voice that spoke louder than words.

Jack guessed that Ryan had made little headway

with getting answers, and he was a little surprised. Though Ryan's work principles matched his own, Ryan was more easy-going. He usually had no trouble in getting people to open up. The fact that he hadn't been able to form a rapport with Walter had Jack wondering about what was causing her to be so cautious. He suddenly sensed it went beyond the normal nerves that most people experienced. Knowing they needed to find some way to put her at ease, Jack considered the best way to proceed. He maintained eye contact with Ryan for only a moment before he turned his attention back to the woman and opened the discussion.

"We appreciate the time you're taking to talk to us," Jack said, keeping his voice low and even in an attempt to get her to relax a little bit.

Walter merely nodded.

"I know all of this must be a little unsettling to you, but we need everybody's help right now so that we can piece together what happened," Jack continued, taking a seat in an empty chair so that they were on eye level.

"I know. It's just that I don't know how I can help," she replied.

"Right now, we're just looking for information. Anything that might lead us in the direction we need to go to find out what happened to the woman we discovered tonight." Jack paused. "Tell us, Ms. Walter, did you notice anything out of the ordinary tonight?"

"Onboard the ship?"

"Onboard this ship, in the surrounding water, by the dock . . ."

A full minute passed before she spoke. "I did see a boat out on the water after we dropped anchor. It was about two hours ago."

"Was there anything about the boat that caught your attention?"

"I didn't see anything specific if that's what you mean, but I heard a splash. At the time I thought it was just jumping fish. But after what you discovered, I'm not sure."

"You heard a splash?"

"Yes."

"How far away was the other boat?" Jack asked, keeping his voice low. He didn't want anybody else to overhear, so that everybody gave their own accounting of what they had observed that night.

Walter lifted a shoulder in a slight shrug. "Maybe about one thousand yards."

"And you're sure you heard a definite splash?"

"Yes."

"Did you recognize anything about the boat that you saw? Any special markings? The name? What type of boat it was?"

"I can't be sure because it was so dark, but it looked like a cabin cruiser."

"They weren't using lights?"

"No. I only recognized its silhouette."

"How long were you outside watching it?"

"Not long at all. As I said, I really didn't think anything about it at the time. I figured it had just dropped anchor and whoever was onboard was just enjoying the night. Much the same as us."

"Did you go back outside after that initial sighting?"

"I did. It was about an hour later. But I'm afraid I couldn't tell you if the boat was still there at the time, or if it had left. I didn't look for it."

Jack was quiet for a moment. "Just out of curiosity, how long have you worked on this ship?"

"A little over a year."

"So you must like being on the water," he said, trying to encourage her to talk.

"I love it. But I'm afraid I mostly work inside. Maybe if I didn't, I would have been more observant tonight," Walter said, her voice containing a hint of apology.

Jack shot her a look of reassurance. "You've been very helpful. We appreciate you taking the time to talk to us."

Walter nodded, and shifted uncomfortably in her chair. "Is it all right if I go now?"

Jack sensed she was anxious for the interview to be over, and he knew there wouldn't be any further information from her, at least at the moment. He reached into his shirt pocket for one of his business cards. "In case you think of anything else, please give me a call. Any time. Day or night."

Walter glanced at the card briefly before tucking it away. "I will."

"Thanks. There's also a chance that we might be contacting you again if we have any further questions."

She nodded and stood. "Then if there's nothing else . . ."

"We're done for now. Thank you," Jack said, watching as she walked away.

Jack waited until she was out of earshot before turning to Ryan. "She was nervous."

"Yeah, she was. It's one of the reasons I wanted to talk to her personally. I didn't want to take any chances that she would totally shut down and not say anything."

"You have no idea on the reason?"

"Not a clue."

Jack grunted and looked around the room at the other interviews. "Do we know if anybody else saw anything yet?"

"Not as far as I know. I told the other police officers helping with the interviews to let me know if anything surfaced. Since nobody has . . ."

"Chances are that nobody else saw anything," Jack concluded grimly.

"That would be my guess."

"It's interesting that Kate heard a splash."

"Yeah, it is. But it might not have anything to do with finding the body. For all we know, it could have just been someone casting a fishing line."

"In the dark? With no lights?"

Ryan lifted a shoulder in a slight shrug. "It's possible."

"Yeah, it is. But the timing and location are suspicious."

"We'll know more once our divers see if they can retrieve anything."

"If the currents haven't already shifted any evidence."

"Finding any evidence in the water is going to be a long shot," Ryan said, rising to his feet. "I'm going to go and talk with the other officers conducting interviews to see if anything else has surfaced."

"While you're doing that, I'm going to go and talk to Ed. I'll fill him in on what we just learned."

## Chapter Three

An hour later, the yacht had docked and the woman's body had been removed and loaded into the back of the coroner's van. The surrounding property had already been taped off, and the police activity was heavy as the coroner's van exited the area.

Jack watched it depart before he went in search of Ashley. He noticed earlier that she had been sitting quietly alone in a corner of the dining salon while people were being interviewed, and he knew that she had been utilizing the skills she had acquired from her days as a newspaper reporter as she watched the questioning process. Though Ashley was taking time off from her career as a reporter to stay at home with their son during his formative years, she still had a tendency to observe people. He wondered if she noticed anything that might help them move forward with the investigation.

Walking into the salon, he saw Ashley sitting in the same spot, while the other guests waited anxiously by the door for permission to leave. Jack walked over to where his wife sat.

"Hey," he said softly as he approached.

Ashley offered him a wan smile. "Hey back."

Jack reached for her hand and squeezed it slightly. "How are you holding up?"

"I think I should be asking you that question. This night turned out a lot different than either one of us expected."

"Ain't that the truth."

"Did anybody see anything?" Ashley asked.

"We might have a lead. One of the employees on the ship admitted to having heard a splash after we dropped anchor. She didn't actually see anything, but she's pretty sure that a cabin cruiser was anchored nearby."

"Was it the red-haired woman I saw you and Ryan talking to earlier?"

Jack looked at her curiously, a little surprised that she had identified the source so quickly. "Yes, it was. Why? Did you notice something about her?"

"She was agitated when she walked away from you two."

"She was nervous when she was talking to us."

"And before. I noticed her immediately once Ryan

got everyone organized in here. The woman went out of her way to push herself to the back of the line. It seemed as if every time it was her turn to talk to the police, she managed to maneuver herself away. It was intentional."

Jack didn't question Ashley's perception. She spent most of her working adult life observing people, chasing a story. Her instincts in reading people were usually very good. "We're going to run a full background check on everyone here tonight. Maybe it'll reveal something about Kate Walter that would explain her nervousness. It's possible that her uneasiness in dealing with the police tonight is stemming from something in her own life."

"Maybe."

"Regardless of what it is, we'll find it," Jack told her just as he heard the shuffle of feet as they started to let people leave. He looked at the crowd briefly before he cast a quick look at his watch. "It's getting late, and your aunt is probably worried. I imagine that the news stations already caught wind that a body was found, and broadcasted it." He had no delusions about the police's ability to keep something like this under wraps.

"You're right. They did."

At Jack's questioning look, she explained, "I called my aunt on my cell phone after we docked. She was watching a local station on television and they broke in with the story. She said that they reported that a body was found in Long Island Sound."

"Did they release any details other than that?"

"No. The station promised an update when information became available."

Jack grunted. "Everything's fine at the house?"

"Yes. My aunt said for us not to worry. John is fast asleep."

"Did he give her any trouble tonight?"

"She said he was an absolute angel."

Jack smiled slightly at the comment. "Why don't you take the car and head on home. It'll be a while before I can leave."

"There's nothing I can do to help?"

"No. Right now, we need to let some pieces of this puzzle fall together. We probably won't know much until we get an identity on the victim."

"If you're sure . . ."

"I am."

Ashley nodded and reached for her purse.

"Do you feel up to driving? If you're tired, I can always arrange for someone to give you a lift," Jack offered.

"It's not necessary. To be honest, with all the commotion going on here tonight, I'm wide awake," she said, beginning to walk beside Jack toward the door.

They had a short wait while the guests from the

party were escorted onto the dock, and Jack noticed that Kate Walter was talking in hushed tones to another member of the crew; a tall, thin man with short, brown hair and hazel eyes. At the moment, the man's broad forehead was creased in a frown.

Jack studied the hand gestures that Walter was making while she spoke, and he watched the two interact. The man Walter was talking to was listening very attentively, and his body language indicated he was a little concerned that they would be overheard. He kept glancing at the people off to his sides, as if he was worried that someone might overhear them.

Jack kept a close eye on the two of them as they were allowed to leave the yacht, and he caught Ryan's eye and motioned him over.

"What's up?" Ryan asked.

"Do we have an ID on the guy talking to Kate Walter?"

Ryan glanced at the couple in question. "His name is Tim Camp. The two of them dated each other a while back."

Jack's eyes narrowed slightly at the news. "They're not seeing each other anymore?"

"No. They broke up about three months ago."

"They're still close," Jack murmured, observing the manner in which Walter rested her hand on Camp's sleeve. He wasn't sure if it was due to a shared secret, or if it was because she needed some sort of reassurance.

"Too close," Ryan murmured as he noticed the gesture. "It doesn't make sense with what we were told about them."

Jack looked at Ryan curiously. "You were speaking to Kate before I came onto the scene. Did she tell you about the relationship she had with Camp?"

"No, but he did. He was concerned that she appeared upset when she was talking to us. He asked if she was okay, and mentioned that they had seen each other a while back. I think it will be interesting to see just what comes in on the background check for the two of them."

"Yes, it will," Jack replied. He heard the sound of footsteps behind him and turned to see Ed. "What's up?" Jack asked, noticing the seriousness of Ed's expression.

"I think we may have an identity on our victim," Ed told them.

"Who?"

"Caryn Cooper. Her stepson Joe works on the ship."

## Chapter Four

"He wasn't working tonight," Jack stated grimly, having already glanced at the list of employees from which they had obtained interviews.

Ed sighed and ran a weary hand through his hair. "I know. But he was supposed to. When McCall gave me the list of employees, he mentioned arbitrarily that Joe Cooper had originally been scheduled to work but he called earlier in the day and said he couldn't due to personal reasons."

"What's the story on the woman?" Ryan asked.

"She was reported missing early this morning by her husband, Sam Cooper. The description that was given to the authorities matches our victim."

"Was the family notified that we found a body?" Jack asked.

"I just sent a car out to meet with them and escort them to the morgue. We'll have to wait to see if they can make a positive ID," Ed answered.

Jack looked at the commotion still going on around them. Though the guests from the party were slowly departing, it seemed as if the crew from the yacht was less enthusiastic to leave. He caught sight of Captain McCall talking to several of his employees. "Did McCall say anything else about Joe Cooper?"

"Just that he's going through a rough patch at the moment. Apparently Joe's father only recently married Caryn and there's been some tension in the family."

Jack frowned. "Did McCall say where the tension's coming from?" He wondered if someone in the Cooper family would have wanted the woman dead.

"He stated that he heard from local gossip that the father might have had second thoughts about the marriage. We'll know more after we talk to them," Ed said, glancing down at his watch. "I think you two should start heading over to the morgue. I'd like you to be there before the Cooper family arrives. I'm hoping that their demeanor might give us some insight as to whether or not they had any involvement in Caryn Cooper's murder."

Jack looked at Ryan. "Ashley was going to take the car. Do you have yours or is Jane taking it?"

"She's catching a lift with Paul Murphy's wife. We can use my car."

"Sounds good," Jack said before turning to Ashley, who was standing quietly off to the side. "Are you sure that you don't want a ride home?"

"It's not necessary. I'll be fine."

"All right. But we'll walk you to the car." Jack looked at Ed. "We'll call you the moment we know something."

Ed nodded. "I'll handle things here while you two are gone."

"We'll see you later."

Thirty minutes later, Jack and Ryan were at the morgue talking to the coroner when two men entered the room. Jack recognized one of the men as Tom Michael, the police officer that had been dispatched to the Cooper residence, but the other man didn't look familiar. Young and of average height and weight, the man had conservatively cut blond hair and a clean-shaven face. Blue eyes that were slightly bloodshot were noticeable behind his wire-framed eyeglasses, and the casual clothes he wore did little to hide the fact that he came from money, as evident by the expensive watch on his wrist and the status insignia on his polo shirt.

Tom escorted the man over to Jack and Ryan. "I'd like to introduce you to Joe Cooper. Mr. Cooper, this is Detective Reeves and Detective Parks."

Jack stepped forward immediately at the introduction, his hand outstretched. "Mr. Cooper, we appreciate you coming down here to meet us."

Joe Cooper shook Jack's hand, his face a mask of anxiety. "I was told that there's a chance that you found my stepmother, Caryn Cooper."

"We found a woman tonight that fits her description. We won't be sure until you ID her."

Joe nodded at Jack's words, but it was the only indication he gave that he heard what was said.

Jack looked at Cooper curiously, noticing the slight ticking of a muscle in his jaw. He got the impression that the man was holding onto his composure by a thread, and he wondered briefly about just how close he had been to his stepmother. Jack's original perception was that the two didn't get along, based on Jim McCall's comment to Ed about tension in the Cooper family. But now he wondered how accurate that was. Glancing briefly at Ryan, Jack turned to the coroner and nodded, indicating that they were ready to see the body.

The coroner immediately escorted them into the bright, white-painted room where the body was being held. Cold, clinical, and sterile, the room seemed to be dominated by the refrigerated drawers that lined one wall, and the metal table where the body lay. The stainless steel cabinetry and workspaces strategically placed around the area did little to detract from the room's purpose, and the change of emotion in Cooper as he caught sight of the draped motionless body was almost tangible. With his eyes transfixed to the table, Cooper walked slowly forward, stopping beside it. He held himself stiffly while the coroner reached for the cloth and lowered it, revealing the first glimpse of the woman.

Jack stood off to the side while Cooper looked at the woman, but he was close enough to see the shock register on the man's facial features. "Do you recognize her?"

Cooper took in a deep, harsh breath. "That's Caryn."

"Are you sure?" Ryan asked.

"I'm positive," Cooper replied, removing his glasses to rub the inside corner of his eyes.

Jack nodded to the coroner, who covered the body before he addressed Cooper. "We're very sorry for your loss."

Cooper didn't respond.

Jack needed to question him, but they also needed him to be in the right frame of mind. "We'd like to ask you some questions if we could."

"Questions?" Cooper repeated as if he was coming out of a daze. He looked at Jack in confusion.

"We realize that this is a difficult time for you, but it's important that we find out about Caryn's lifestyle. The sooner the better. We need to determine exactly what happened to her."

Total silence followed Jack's comment, and it was a full minute before Cooper responded. "I'll try and help."

"We appreciate that. There's a conference room at the end of the hall we can use. Why don't we go there to talk."

"All right."

Jack led the way to the room and waited until Cooper was seated at the table. "Before we begin, can we get you a cup of coffee or something to drink?"

"Coffee."

Jack turned to Ryan. "Do you mind getting it?"

"I'll be right back." Ryan returned moments later and placed the cup before Cooper on the table. "I'm afraid I can't vouch for how good it is."

"I'm sure it's fine," Cooper replied, taking a sip.

Jack watched Cooper, trying to get a reading on him. He knew that often times, people's actions spoke louder than any words could. "We know that the questions we'll be asking will be difficult for you to answer considering what happened, but let me assure you that we'll stop for a break whenever you need one." Jack noticed that Cooper sat stiffly in his chair, his hands wrapped tightly around the coffee. "Is there anybody that you'd like us to contact?" he asked, trying to give the man time to settle in.

Cooper took another sip of his coffee before responding. "No."

"What about your father?" Jack pressed, not understanding why the man didn't accompany his son.

Cooper shook his head slightly. "No. My father is extremely upset right now. He wanted to come with me, but his doctor advised against it. My father has a bad heart and we're all a little concerned about how he's going to handle all this. Considering everything, I think it would be best if I told him in person."

"Dealing with something of this magnitude is extremely difficult," Jack sympathized. Cooper was beginning to talk a little more freely, and Jack wanted to make sure that he understood that they were on his side.

Cooper took another sip. "I don't think I've ever seen my father this distraught."

Jack didn't say anything in response, he couldn't. There was nothing he could say that would help. Instead, he tried to refocus the conversation back to Caryn Cooper. "We understand that your stepmother was reported missing early this morning. Was she at home last night?"

"She was. I had dinner with my father and Caryn around seven o'clock and then they went to bed."

"About what time was that?"

"Around eight-thirty."

"Do they normally turn in so early?" Ryan asked.

"It's not unusual."

"You didn't see either of them after that time?"

"No," Cooper responded, continuing to cradle the coffee cup between his palms, his eyes downcast to the table. "I was meeting some friends last night, and I left shortly after they turned in."

"Who did you meet with?" Jack asked.

"Just some people I work with."

"Can you be more specific?"

"Kate Walter and Tim Camp."

Jack's interest piqued. "Were you with them all night?"

"No. I left them around twelve-thirty or so. I'm in the process of getting my MBA, and I had a class the next morning."

"Just out of curiosity, where did you go when you met your friends?"

Joe lifted a shoulder in a slight shrug. "Just to the Sand Pit," he said, naming a dance club on the North Shore.

There was no hesitation by Cooper to reveal information, so Jack moved on with his questioning. He knew he would be verifying Cooper's claims later. "Did everything seem normal between your father and Caryn last night? Was there any tension in the air? Had they argued about anything?"

Cooper shook his head and raised his eyes. "Not that I noticed. Our family has our share of problems but there wasn't anything that would have caused Caryn to leave my father."

Cooper's comment caused Jack to look at him curiously. "Is that what you think happened? That Caryn left the house on her own free will?"

Cooper looked surprised by the question. "She had to. She was missing when my father awoke this morning."

"What time was that?" Ryan asked.

"Around four o'clock. He's always been an early riser. He woke me immediately when he discovered that Caryn was gone."

"You live at home?"

"Yes. The house is large enough where we don't get in each other's way."

Jack considered the statement. "How would you categorize your relationship with your stepmother?"

Cooper shrugged. "We got along okay if that's what you're asking."

"There wasn't any sort of tension between the two of you?"

"Not anything that I wouldn't consider normal," Cooper said, pausing for a moment. "I'm not going to lie. When my father first introduced me to Caryn, I was a little leery of her. She was much younger than he was, and I began to wonder about her motive in marrying him. I thought perhaps she was with him for his money."

"And that bothered you."

"It would bother anybody," Cooper stated. "I wasn't thrilled with my father's choice, but I also know he has the right to be with whoever he wants."

"That must have been hard though. Living in the same house as them when you didn't fully approve of their relationship."

"I'm only going to be there until I graduate. I went back to school full-time, so living at the house made financial sense."

"I take it by that comment that you found a way to co-exist with them," Jack remarked.

"I did. To be honest, I had even begun to like Caryn. She made my father happy, which I guess is all anybody could ask for . . ."

When he wouldn't continue, Jack said, "We appreciate your honesty."

"I want to help in any way I can."

"Can you tell us if there was anyone who would have wanted to see Caryn harmed? Did she have any problems with anybody? Was there anyone she had recently argued with?"

"Not that I know of."

"If Caryn was having problems, is that something she would have shared with you?" Ryan asked.

"She never sought me out to have a heart-to-heart conversation, but she sometimes mentioned things that bothered her. Though to be honest, I think it was more of a way for her to vent."

"What do you mean?"

Cooper shrugged. "Just that I don't think she was

looking to me for advice. She was really just talking aloud. I think she was grateful that she had someone who would listen."

Jack couldn't help but wonder why the woman would seek Cooper out, instead of her husband. "She didn't talk to your father about things that bothered her?"

"She would only talk to him if she had a problem that she needed help with. My father has a tendency to want to fix things. I speak from experience when I say that sometimes you don't want or need anyone to 'fix' your problems. You only want someone to listen, someone to bounce things off of."

Jack understood that. "Do you know if she discussed any problems with your father recently?"

"No. But to be honest, my father isn't the type of person that talks about his personal life. I can pretty much guarantee that he would keep whatever Caryn told him in confidence."

"It sounds like he was devoted to her," Ryan commented.

"He was."

"We're going to need to talk to him personally," Jack told him. "Do you think he'll be up to it tonight?"

Cooper shook his head. "To be honest, I don't know. He's taking all of this very hard."

"We understand. But if it's okay with you, we'd like to try. You need a ride home from here. Why don't we take you and see if your father is willing to talk to us."

Cooper stared at him for a long moment. "I'll call my father before we leave and let him know you're coming."

"We'd appreciate that."

## Chapter Five

The Cooper household was lit like a beacon as Jack, Ryan, and Joe Cooper drove up. The sprawling brick ranch home's circular driveway was lined with cars, and people were entering and leaving the residence in a steady flow.

Jack glanced to the back of the car at Cooper. The man had been quiet on the drive over but Jack heard his restless movements as they neared his home. "It looks like you have company."

Cooper was frowning as he watched the proceedings at the house. "I guess my father's friends heard about a body being found," he said, reaching for the door handle as soon as the car came to a complete stop. "I'd better get inside. My father was pretty distraught when I left the house. I don't think he's up to dealing with people."

"You don't think he invited these people over?" Jack asked, opening his own car door and stepping out into the humid night air.

"I doubt it. My father has never been much of a socializer. That was Caryn's department. As reticent as he is, Caryn was the complete opposite. She loved being the life of the party."

Jack frowned. "Did she ever go out on her own at night? Did she have a crowd that she hung out with?"

"Sometimes," Cooper admitted as a thought occurred to him. "Do you think that one of the people that Caryn considered her friend was responsible for her murder?"

"Unfortunately, we can't rule it out," Ryan answered as he walked over to Jack and Cooper. He glanced at the row of cars. "Earlier you had stated that you didn't know of any problems that Caryn may have had with anybody. Can you think of the names of any of her friends that she may have mentioned recently in passing? Any one of them that she may have met with? It's possible that they might be able to help us piece together what happened."

Cooper began walking up the stone path that led to the front door. "To be honest, Caryn never spoke with me about her friends. And quite frankly, I didn't spend much time in her social circle. Other than attending a few quiet dinner parties that my father and Caryn had at the house, I never really had the opportunity to meet many of Caryn's friends."

"You never overheard Caryn arguing with anybody over the phone?" Jack asked.

"No. As I think I mentioned earlier, Caryn and I weren't that close. For the most part, school and my job took up most of my time. We really didn't spend too much time in each other's company. If we were in the house together, we were usually in separate rooms." Cooper fell silent as he opened the front door and stepped into the house. All eyes turned to him.

Jack saw the way Cooper stiffened as his eyes searched the room, and he watched his fists clench as an older man that bore a strong resemblance to him walked carefully across the room to where they stood. Jack surmised it was Sam Cooper. He had the same shock of blond hair, the same build, the same facial features, and blue eyes. But where Joe Cooper's face was tan and unlined, Sam Cooper's skin showed the ravage of time.

"Dad, this is Detective Reeves and Detective Parks," Joe said.

Sam barely acknowledged Jack and Ryan. His attention was on his son. "Was it Caryn?"

"I'm sorry, Dad," Joe told him quietly, then reached out to offer support when he practically crumpled before them.

Jack immediately stepped forward to assist him.

Sam looked at Jack. "What happened to Caryn?" he asked, his voice breaking on the question.

"That's what we're going to find out," Jack said. "Is there somewhere we can talk in private?"

Sam held Jack's gaze for a moment before he slowly nodded.

Jack glanced at Ryan. "Do you want to stay here?" he asked, with the unspoken message that he should try and see if there were any leads from any of the people in the house that might explain how Caryn Cooper ended up dead.

"Yeah," Ryan replied.

Jack nodded and, with a questioning look to Joe Cooper, followed Joe and Sam to a quiet room where they could talk.

After they settled in a home office, Jack leaned forward, his hands clasped by his knees. "Mr. Cooper, I know this is an extremely difficult time for you right now, and I'm sorrier than I could say that you have to go through this. But I need to ask you some questions if I could."

Sam lifted lifeless eyes to meet Jack's. "I understand."

Jack held the man's gaze, hoping the responses he got from Sam were said with a clear head. "I'll stop the questioning anytime you feel the need for a break."

"Thank you."

Joe interrupted the small exchange and looked at his father with concern. "Before Detective Reeves begins, can I get you something, Dad? Do you want something to drink?"

Sam shook his head. He focused on Jack. "What did you need to know?"

"For starters, do you know of anybody that would have wanted to see your wife dead?"

"No. As far as I know, all of Caryn's friends thought very highly of her. You can see by the amount of people here tonight that everybody was concerned about her disappearance."

"How did they find out about it?" Jack asked curiously.

"This morning when I discovered Caryn missing, I called around, asking if anybody had seen her. As soon as the story broke on the news that a body of a woman had been discovered, our friends started calling and stopping by. We were all hoping that the body discovered wouldn't be Caryn."

Jack nodded. The fact that their friends wanted to offer moral support was no surprise. "You're lucky to have good friends."

"Yes, Caryn was a good woman."

"Your son mentioned that you and your wife went to bed early last night."

"We did. We had a hectic schedule yesterday, and we were looking forward to a good night's sleep."

"What do you mean by hectic schedule? Did you do anything unusual?"

"My wife volunteered to work on a fitness committee at the gym she attends. Their goal is to get people involved with health and fitness. They had raised money to build a new facility for the underprivileged in the community, and she had talked me into becoming involved with the cause. Yesterday, we had a couple of meetings with several suppliers regarding exercise equipment that we were trying to get donated."

"That sounds like an ambitious venture."

"It is. It's never easy to get people to donate anything unless they believe it's to their benefit. Caryn spent most of the time meeting with the suppliers and assuring them that the publicity they received from their donations would benefit the bottom line of their company."

"I imagine that's rewarding work."

Sam smiled slightly. "Caryn had a competitive streak by nature. She loved the challenge of getting people to agree to her way of thinking. She was very good at putting on the charm."

Jack studied Sam curiously, noticing the way the man's features softened as he spoke of his wife. "It sounds as if she charmed you," he said gently.

"She did. I met Caryn under similar circumstances about six months ago. I own a couple of hardware stores, and she asked for a meeting one day. She was trying to get me to donate tools for another one of her projects. She was on a committee that was trying to build a playground at one of the local non-profit children centers. It was a place where kids of single working parents could be safe after school. A place where they could mingle with their friends under adult supervision, and their parents wouldn't have to worry about what they were up to. Caryn had volunteered to head the committee to get local businesses to provide the materials necessary for the project."

"Has she always been involved in that sort of thing? Helping to improve the community?"

"Yes. But she took on a more active role after the death of her first husband."

"She was a widow?" Jack asked, somewhat surprised.

"Yes. She was married to a man by the name of Roger Camp."

"How long was she widowed?"

"Eight months."

"So you and Caryn got together fairly quickly after his death."

Sam nodded. "We had a whirlwind courtship. She was a recent widow who couldn't handle being alone, and I was a long time widower tired of being alone. We had a lot in common. She needed somebody and I needed to be needed."

"Just out of curiosity, how did her first husband die?"

"He had a heart attack."

Jack looked over at Joe Cooper. "Is Roger Camp any relation to Tim Camp, your co-worker?"

"Roger was Tim's father," Joe responded.

Jack leaned back in his chair. He had a sudden flashback to earlier that evening when he saw Kate Walter talking to Tim Camp before disembarking from the yacht. At the time, he had thought that they were uneasy about something, as if they were hiding something. He suddenly wondered if that was true. "How close was Tim to Caryn?"

"Not close at all," Sam replied. "Tim's parents had a bitter divorce and his mother had full custody of him. As far as I know, Tim didn't see his father much."

"Any idea why?"

"His parents just didn't get along. To be honest, I don't think that they could be in the same room with each other without arguing."

"So rather than cause further problems, Roger Camp stayed out of his son's life?"

"Yes," Sam said, pausing for a moment. "And unfortunately, I think Tim blamed Caryn for both the breakup of his parents' marriage and Roger staying out of Tim's life."

"Why?"

Sam hesitated before admitting, "Caryn became

friends with Roger before his divorce with Tim's mother. And while the marriage was all but over before Caryn came on the scene, I'm not sure if Tim understood that."

"Meaning he thought that Roger left his mother for Caryn?"

"Yes."

Jack considered he might have come across a motive for Caryn Cooper's death. Tim Camp could have held a lot of resentment against Caryn, especially if he blamed her for his father not being around for him. If he blamed her for his father leaving his mother. "Did Caryn ever talk about Roger Camp with you?"

Sam gave a slight shrug. "Just the information I told you. We pretty much stayed off the topic of our past relationships."

"Why?"

"Jealousy."

Jack kept his face expressionless, even though he knew the man's answer was important. The fact that he admitted that there was jealousy within the relationship was an admission that they had problems. "On Caryn's part or yours?"

"Mine."

## Chapter Six

"You were jealous," Jack said, careful to keep his tone neutral. He didn't want the man to think that his responses were being used to determine the possibility of his guilt in his wife's murder.

Sam Cooper ran a shaky hand down his face. "I'm ashamed to say that I was jealous of my wife's relationships. Past and present. It bothered me to think of her meeting with the suppliers for her charity projects, all of whom were men."

"Did Caryn ever give you any reason to feel threatened?"

"No, I'm afraid it's an emotion that just came naturally. My wife was a very beautiful woman. A very outgoing, friendly woman. Almost the exact opposite of myself. I enjoyed staying home nights and she enjoyed going to parties and socializing. I couldn't help but think that she resented being with me sometimes. She would have enjoyed herself more with someone whose personality was more closely related to hers."

Jack looked at him curiously. "You sound very sure of that. Did she ever say that outright?"

"No, she wouldn't. It wasn't in her nature. She was very gracious, very careful not to say anything that anybody would take offense to."

"Did you ever fight about staying home at night?"

"Fight?" Sam repeated, pausing for a moment to collect his thoughts. "I wouldn't exactly say that."

"What would you say?"

"I would say we had a difference of opinion on how to spend our evenings."

"Did you have a difference of opinion last night on how to spend the evening?"

"No, last night we were in total agreement."

"Yet your wife was missing when you awoke."

Joe Cooper cast a sharp look at Jack. "Caryn often went for early morning jogs, and she was found in running clothes. Surely that would imply that she wasn't out partying."

Jack nodded. "It would. However, it doesn't preclude the possibility that she left to meet someone. And unless you noticed anything this morning that would suggest Caryn was taken against her will, that's the scenario we have to consider." He let his words sink in. "Did you notice anything out of the ordinary when you awoke this morning?"

Sam was shaking his head before Jack finished. "No, but there was no note in the kitchen, either."

"Would she have left a note?"

"She always had in the past."

The statement drew Jack's full attention. "What do you mean by that?"

"Sometimes if she was having difficulty sleeping, she would go off on an early morning run. But she always left a note . . ."

Jack watched the man quietly for a moment, wondering how his next words would be perceived. "Mr. Cooper, we need to search your house. Maybe there's a clue that will help us piece together what happened to Caryn."

"Search the house?" Joe Cooper repeated, frowning slightly.

Jack looked at him. "It's standard procedure," he assured him, curious if he was going to give them a fight over it. It would be immaterial. Regardless of whether or not the Coopers agreed, a thorough search of the house would be completed as soon as they had a search warrant in hand. Jack knew that Ryan would have already been on the phone getting the proper paperwork together.

Sam looked at his son. "It's okay. If the authorities

can find anything that would tell us what happened to Caryn, they have my full authorization to do whatever they need to."

"But—"

"It's fine, Joe," Sam said. "As Detective Reeves stated, this is standard procedure."

Joe looked at his father for a brief moment longer before slowly nodding.

Jack's gaze encompassed both men. "We appreciate your cooperation. I'm going to go and talk to my partner, Detective Parks. He should have already been in contact with the station to get a search team out here. With any luck, we'll find something that will give us a lead on what happened to Caryn."

Sam nodded. "What can Joe and I do to help?"

"We need to clear out your friends that are here. I know they mean well, but it's imperative that we get them out of the house while the search is going on."

"We'll handle that," Joe assured him.

"There is one other thing that I need you to do."

"What?"

"I'm going to need a list of names, addresses, and phone numbers of all of Caryn's friends and acquaintances, including anyone she worked with on any committees. I'd like a notation placed next to the name of anybody who showed up here tonight."

"Do you think that one of these people had something to do with Caryn's death?" Sam asked.

Jack heard the concern in the question. "I'm afraid right now, we can't rule anything out."

"But they were Caryn's friends."

"In which case, they should all be cleared as possible suspects. But on the off chance that somebody out there might know something, we need to take all necessary precautions to ensure that nothing slips through the cracks."

"I'll get you the list," Joe murmured, knowing that his father might be too upset to do it.

"Thank you," Jack said, rising to his feet. "I'm going to go and make sure that everything is in place."

Joe nodded. "My father and I will be out in a minute."

"All right." Jack couldn't help but wonder if they knew something about Caryn's death that they weren't saying.

"We won't be long," Sam assured him.

"I'll be right outside."

Jack noticed Ryan immediately as he stepped into the still crowded living room. He was by the front door talking to a uniformed police officer. Jack walked over.

Ryan looked up. "The search team should be here soon," he assured Jack.

"You got the warrant?"

Ryan held up a piece of paper. "Officer Smith just brought it. Ed had a judge on standby waiting for the ID on the woman." He looked over at the closed door of the study. "Where are the Coopers?"

"They needed a few minutes alone. They should be out shortly. They promised their full cooperation with the search."

"How are they handling Caryn's death?" Ryan asked.

"Sam Cooper is taking it hard. His son, Joe, is a little more calm at the moment."

"Did either of them balk at the search?"

"Joe did a little. I'm not sure yet if it was because he has something to hide, or if it's because he doesn't know what to expect."

"I guess we'll find out." Ryan gestured to the direction Jack had just come from. "Here they are now."

Jack turned. "Everything okay?"

"Yes," Sam replied. "You can get started on the search at any time."

"Why don't we get the guests cleared out first."

"I'll take care of it," Joe said. "My father will take you up to the bedroom that he and Caryn shared. I think if there's anything that might give any clues about what happened to Caryn, it will probably be there."

"What makes you say that?" Jack asked.

"Because that's where Caryn's personal items are. We have a small sitting room off of the bedroom that was converted to an office. Caryn claimed it as hers," Sam told him.

Jack looked at Ryan. "Why don't I head up with

Mr. Cooper? You can stay here and help Joe clear out the house."

"Not a problem."

Jack nodded at Ryan's assurance and turned back to Sam. "Why don't we get started."

## Chapter Seven

An hour later, the search of the Cooper residence was well under way. The entire house had been canvassed by the search team, and boxes and paper bags filled with possible evidence were being logged and carted off to the vans that waited outside. Though their search of Caryn's office didn't reveal anything, the files in her computer would be reviewed to see if there was anything that might shed some light on her murder, and the phone records would also be looked at.

As her computer and cell phone were taken into evidence, Jack took a brief moment to go in search of Ryan. He found him in Sam Cooper's study, the same area where Jack had originally spoken to the man.

"Find anything yet?" Jack asked, watching as Ryan sorted through some files from the desk.

Ryan didn't look up at the question. "Maybe. I'm not sure."

"What do you mean?" Jack walked over to Ryan.

"Take a look," Ryan said, handing over a few sheets of paper he had pulled from some files.

"This is information on Roger Camp, Caryn's first husband," Jack said, looking at a copy of the certificate of her first marriage, as well as the man's death certificate and insurance policy.

"Why do you suppose Sam Cooper would keep a file like that?" Ryan asked.

"I'm not sure." Jack noted the amount of the insurance policy value: Two hundred and fifty thousand dollars. "According to what he told me earlier, he and Caryn were careful to keep each other's past relationships out of their conversations. He admitted that he had a problem with jealousy."

"That might explain why he has the papers in his possession then."

Jack's eyes narrowed slightly. "An obsession with her past?"

"It's possible."

"Yeah, it is. But there's also a chance that the man is interested in the financial gain from the policy," Jack said, realizing that if Caryn was out of the picture, any monies she held in her name would in all likelihood revert to Sam.

"Did he give any indication that he's in financial trouble?" Ryan asked curiously.

"No, but with a little research we should be able to determine that."

"It's a possible motive."

"Yes. But there's also another possible suspect."

"Who?"

"Do you remember the guy we saw talking to Kate Walter when she was waiting to leave the ship?" Jack asked.

Ryan's forehead creased in a frown. "His last name was Camp. Tim Camp. Is he any relation to Roger Camp?"

"It's his son. And from what I was told, Roger's and Tim's relationship wasn't solid, and Tim had a lot of resentment against Caryn for it."

"You'll have to fill me in on everything later."

Jack promised to just as the door to the study opened and Sam Cooper walked in.

Cooper paused as he noticed Jack and Ryan by his desk. His expression revealed a brief moment of panic before he got it under control. "Are you looking for anything in particular?"

Jack motioned to the chair in front of the desk. "Why don't you have a seat, Mr. Cooper."

He slowly did as Jack suggested. "Is this about those documents?" He motioned to the papers with his chin.

"It is. We have a couple of questions for you if you don't mind."

"What did you want to know?"

"We're curious. Why are you holding onto these documents? You gave me the impression earlier that you and Caryn kept your past relationships private," Jack said.

"We did. At least as far as not bringing it up in conversation. But neither one of us lived in a cocoon. All of our financial matters were handled by my broker. Caryn didn't have her own."

"So you took full responsibility for investing her money?" Ryan asked.

"If that's what you want to call it."

There was something about the way that Cooper made the comment, an inflection in his voice that had Jack looking at him curiously. "Could you explain what you mean by that?"

Cooper leaned back in his chair. "There's something I didn't say to you earlier. Something that I don't want my son to know."

"Your son's not here now," Jack said.

Realizing that the man might need further assurance, Jack said, "Mr. Cooper, whatever you say to us, stays between us. Nobody will find out, at least through our sources."

Cooper's eyes met Jack's. "I appreciate that." He let out an expressive sigh. "I'm not trying to be difficult, please believe me. It's just that this is a hard topic for me to talk about."

"I understand. But it's important that you be totally honest with us."

Cooper was quiet for a long moment. "My wife's first husband had a lot of debts."

"That's nothing out of the ordinary. A lot of people have debt," Ryan said.

"That's true. But most people aren't in debt to the extent that Roger Camp was. The man was a gambler. A heavy gambler. The horse track, poker, Atlantic City, you name it, and he was involved. Especially if the stakes were high."

"And that's where his debt accumulated?" Jack questioned.

"Mostly from there, but also from some bad investments. Roger tried to recoup some of his money by risky ventures. In essence, if there was a chance of a big payoff, he took the risk."

"And the risks never panned out," Ryan murmured, having an idea of where this was going.

"No. When he died, he owed roughly three million. The money that Caryn received from his life insurance went toward paying some of his debt."

Jack studied Cooper curiously. "If he owed three million dollars, the money from the insurance policy wouldn't even make a dent in the debt."

"No, you're right. It didn't. I've been negotiating with them since I married Caryn, and I finally got his creditors to agree to accept two million dollars as payment in full."

"Meaning you put up the additional money," Jack deduced.

Cooper nodded. "I thought it would be in everybody's best interest to get the matter settled quickly."

Jack tried to determine how truthful Cooper was being. It bothered him that Cooper didn't mention anything about this earlier. Regardless of what he didn't want his son to know, it didn't make sense that he would keep something of this magnitude to himself, especially considering what had happened to his wife. "Do you think the people that Roger owed money to had something to do with Caryn's death?"

"I'm not sure. I had thought that I had everything under control."

"When did the money change hands?"

"A few weeks ago. It was handled through a bank wire. I'm not even sure who the money went to. Everything was handled through a third party."

"Did anybody else know about this?" Ryan asked,

Cooper shook his head. "No. Caryn and I didn't want too many people involved. We figured the less people who knew, the better. We didn't want to upset anyone."

"Meaning?" Jack prompted.

"Meaning my son, Joe. He wouldn't have understood. I'm afraid he always thought that Caryn only married me for my money. And though that was never true, this would only have validated that theory."

Jack made a mental note of the comment. "After

you made the payment toward the debt, did anybody try and contact you again?"

"No. I thought everything was settled. But after what happened to Caryn, now I'm not sure that it was."

"Did you keep the records of the transfer?"

"I did." Cooper stood up and walked over to the bookcase and removed a panel, revealing a wall safe. He quickly opened it. Removing an envelope, he handed it to Jack. "This is everything."

Jack briefly looked at the documents before handing them to Ryan. "We'll have our own people go through everything. It's possible we'll be able to trace who the money went to."

"They promised that they would leave Caryn alone."

"Your wife's death may have nothing to do with the money her first husband owed," Ryan said, placing the papers he had just reviewed onto the desktop. "Don't worry, Mr. Cooper. We'll find out who killed your wife."

Cooper's attention diverted to sounds of shuffling coming from the hallway as items uncovered during the search were removed from the home.

Jack noticed the man's preoccupation with the search. "Mr. Cooper, if you have somewhere else you can go to get some rest, it might be better. The search team has a lot more ground to cover."

"I'd like to stay," he said.

"It's your choice."

"Is there anything else I can do to help?"

"Not right now. Unless you have any more safes in the house where your wife might have stored papers . . ."

Cooper motioned to the bookcase. "That's the only one."

"If you want to stay, you'll need to allow the search team to do their job without interference."

"I will," Cooper assured him before turning toward the door. "I'm going to go and find my son. Call me if you have any further questions."

"We will. We do appreciate how cooperative you've been."

Cooper paused in the open doorway and looked back at Jack and Ryan. "I want you to find out what happened to my wife."

## Chapter Eight

Several hours later, Jack and Ryan were back at the port where the *Aphrodite* was docked. The area had been barricaded to keep anybody not associated with the investigation from interfering, and a small section in front of the gated entrance had been set up for a press conference that was underway. At the moment, the reporters were shouting unrelenting questions to the police spokesman.

Jack looked at the structured chaos. "It didn't take long for this to become a three-ring circus."

"It never does," Ryan replied.

Jack flashed his badge as he and Ryan walked through one of the checkpoints and over to the underwater search and recovery unit, where Ed was talking to one of the officers.

Ed saw Jack and excused himself from the officer.

"Did the underwater search and recovery unit come up with anything?" Jack asked.

"Not yet. They're working with underwater lights, but it's tough going. Even with the coordinates we received from McCall, the search area has to be pretty wide due to the shifting currents."

"What about the crew from McCall's yacht? Did anybody remember anything after Ryan and I left?"

Ed put his hands in his pockets and rocked back on his heels. "Actually, somebody did. Tim Camp suddenly recalled seeing a boat floating near the yacht. His story pretty much matches Kate Walter's."

"That's interesting," Ryan murmured.

"Especially since we saw the two of them whispering to each other once the yacht docked," Jack said.

"You think there's some type of collaboration going on between the two of them?" Ed questioned.

"I think it's entirely possible, especially after what we found out at the Coopers'. Tim Camp's father Roger was married to Caryn Cooper. He was her first husband," Ryan revealed.

Ed frowned. "Where's Roger Camp now? Did we send someone over to talk to him?"

"We can't. He's dead."

"How did he die?"

"Heart attack."

"What kind of relationship did the guy have with his son?" Ed asked.

Jack a shrugged. "From what we were able to determine, not much of one."

"So there could have been some resentment on Tim Camp's part against Caryn Cooper."

"It's possible. Even likely."

"Maybe even enough to give him a motive to want Caryn Cooper dead," Ed suggested. "How was Roger Camp set financially prior to his death?"

"He wasn't," Jack replied. "He was in heavy debt. We'll fill you in on all the details later."

Ed nodded. "Do you think Tim Camp was aware of the situation?"

"It's doubtful," Ryan replied. "When we spoke to Sam Cooper back at the house, I got the impression that nobody was aware of just how desperate Roger Camp's situation had become."

Ed looked at Jack. "What about you? Did you get the same impression?"

"I did."

"Then considering the fact that nothing was released to the press about Caryn Cooper missing, and that we didn't have an ID on the body when we interviewed McCall's employees, there's no reason why Kate Walter and Tim Camp should have been trying to corroborate any stories. Not unless they were trying to cover up something."

"Which is the impression they gave," Ryan told him.

"To be honest, I think it's immaterial that no information was released on Caryn Cooper's disappearance," Jack said.

"Why do you say that?" Ed asked.

"Because there was a crowd at the Cooper residence when we arrived. I think that everybody within their social circle knew about Caryn's disappearance."

"There was that much activity at the house?" Ed asked.

"Yeah."

"Just out of curiosity, how was Joe Cooper behaving? Was there any reluctance on his part to talk to us?"

"Nothing that I would categorize as out of the ordinary. He didn't fall over himself offering to help, but he didn't protest when his father made the decision to cooperate fully. Joe even supplied us a list of Caryn's friends, and he made a notation of which ones were at the house when we got there."

"How many people were there?" Ed asked.

"About ten. It will at least give us a starting point when we start interviewing people."

"Yeah, but that means that anybody who was there will have had the time to consider their answers before speaking to us," Ed said just as the two-way radio he held signaled.

"What do we have?" Ed asked into the receiver without preamble.

"An old anchor."

## Chapter Nine

Dawn was just breaking as Jack walked into his house. Carefully closing the front door so that he wouldn't disturb Ashley and John, he shrugged out of his suit jacket, relieved that he could finally take a breather. He was exhausted.

The long hours already spent on Caryn Cooper's murder investigation had taken a toll physically and mentally. The anchor that the underwater search and recovery unit had pulled from the floor of Long Island Sound was proof that someone tried to dispose of Caryn Cooper's body. The catch of an ankle bracelet had become imbedded in the pitted rusted metal of the anchor, and Sam Cooper had identified the piece of jewelry as one that he had given Caryn while they were dating.

"Jack?" a soft voice asked from the stairwell above.

Jack looked up, his expression softening as he caught sight of Ashley staring down at him from the shadows. "Hi, babe."

"Are you okay?" she asked, moving away from the railing to walk down the stairs.

Jack met her halfway. "Just tired." He enfolded her in his arms and hugged her tight.

Ashley returned the embrace. "Did you find out anything about the woman? Did you get an identity?"

"Her name is Caryn Cooper."

"The name's familiar."

"Is it?" Jack released her and looked at her curiously, inviting her to continue. Ashley always seemed to have her pulse on the current events of the area. She always seemed to know everything that was going on. Her natural curiosity and her old reporter instincts ensured that she paid attention to details that other people might overlook.

"If I'm not mistaken, she was heavily involved in charities."

Since Ashley's statement substantiated what Jack had been told by Sam Cooper, he asked, "What did you read about her?"

"I know she was involved with the fitness committee at the gym on Main Street."

"Anything else?"

Ashley thought for a moment. "Maybe. There was a recent newspaper article about a fund-raising luncheon for the new gym that Caryn Cooper attended. The paper listed some of the names of the guests. One of them was James McCall."

Jack frowned. "McCall? That was the name of our ship's captain."

"I know. But I would imagine that McCall is a common name. There's a chance that it's not the same person. He was with you when you pulled the body from the water. Did he recognize her?"

"He didn't say anything at the time, or when we interviewed him for that matter."

"What about his facial expression? Was there any indication that he knew who she was?"

"Unfortunately, my full concentration was on the body, not McCall. I couldn't actually say whether or not he expressed any recognition."

"There were a lot of people outside with you. It's possible that one of them noticed his reaction."

"It is." Jack left Ashley's side and walked over to the phone to dial Ed's cell. After a few minutes of conversation, he disconnected the call. "Ed will double check to see if anybody noticed anything strange with McCall. We should have an answer to the question later on today."

"I'll make some calls to some of my contacts down at the newspaper. I should be able to verify if the James McCall that was in attendance at the luncheon is the same man that owns the *Aphrodite*."

"Be careful not to let on about your reason for asking," Jack cautioned, knowing that if it did turn out to be the same person, McCall would have to be investigated as a suspect. If that was the case, he didn't want to tip the guy off that Ashley helped put him in that position.

Ashley shot him a wry look. "Have I failed you before?"

"No," Jack replied, a slight smile hovering on his lips.

"And I won't now."

"I know you won't. Can you recall anything else?"

"Not offhand, but I'll see what I can come up with. The project had been getting a lot of press coverage. Of course it's all been reported in the Life section of the newspaper, which might explain why you haven't made the connection." Ashley knew Jack rarely paid attention to those type of articles. If it wasn't hardcore news, her husband pretty much ignored other sections.

"I'd appreciate any help you can offer."

"I'll check with some contacts I have at the newspaper." She looked at the clock. "Are you hungry? Can I fix you something to eat?"

"No thanks. I just want to get something to drink. If it's all the same to you, I'd rather just go to bed after that. I'd like to get to the police station by noon so that I can start reviewing the evidence."

"Why don't you head up and do what you need to do. I'll bring up the drink. Is orange juice okay?"

"Sounds good. Thanks."

"No problem. I'll be up in a few minutes," Ashley said, turning to walk into the kitchen.

Jack watched her go before walking upstairs. Once he reached the landing, he headed toward his son's bedroom. Though the room was dimly lit by a night-light, he could clearly see John sleeping. The sight brought a sense of peace over him. No matter how frustrated his job made him, coming home to Ashley and John made it all worthwhile.

He had been standing in the doorway looking at his son's sleeping form when he sensed Ashley walk up behind him. He felt her arm wrap around his waist as she handed him the small glass of juice.

"Thanks," Jack murmured, lifting the glass to his lips while his free arm made its way around her waist. "How was John when you got home?"

Ashley smiled and leaned into him. "He was sound asleep and so was my aunt."

"Did she stay the night?"

"No. She wanted to go home. I told her she was more than welcome to stay, but she was just as determined to leave. I think she had a meeting with her garden club mid–morning. Maybe she was afraid that if she stayed here she would miss it."

Ashley nudged Jack. "If we're lucky, John will sleep a few more hours. I know my aunt wore him out by playing with him. Why don't we try and take advantage of the peace and quiet and head off to bed."

Jack smiled at Ashley's comment, knowing that the moment John awoke he would be a whirlwind of activity. "Sounds like a good idea." He cast a final look at John and turned to walk to their bedroom, Ashley held close to his side.

## Chapter Ten

It was close to noon when Jack made his way into the police station and over to Ed's office. Knocking once on the closed door, he didn't wait for an invitation to let himself in.

Ed leaned back in his chair. "I'm glad you're here," he said by way of greeting.

"Did we come up with anything new?" Jack asked, taking a seat across the desk from Ed.

"I was able to confirm that Jim McCall, our ship's captain, knew Caryn Cooper, and not just by name," Ed replied grimly.

"But he didn't admit that on his own," Jack guessed, recalling that the man had expressed nothing at the time the body was pulled onto the yacht that indicated he knew the woman.

"Hardly. He was still hanging around the area when you called me this morning, so I took the opportunity to confront him. To say he was a little disconcerted that we made the connection so quickly would be an understatement."

"I can imagine his reaction. What did he say after you challenged him about knowing her?"

"Not much. He tried to convince me that his physical contact with Caryn Cooper was minimal. He stated that there was no way that he could have made the identification because he only met her a few times."

"You didn't believe him."

"No," Ed replied, reaching for a manila folder that he handed to Jack. "Take a look."

Inside was a photograph of the luncheon Ashley had mentioned. McCall stood directly beside Caryn Cooper.

"Look at the other photos in the folder," Ed instructed.

Jack quickly glanced at the nine remaining photographs. Each one depicted Jim McCall and Caryn Cooper. In a few, the two were seen laughing together about something. "This doesn't look like their contact was minimal."

"No, it doesn't. You have to admit, the photographs shine a lot of suspicion on the man. Caryn Cooper's body wasn't marked or bruised in any way that would have made her unrecognizable."

"No, you're right. Her stepson Joe had no problem identifying the remains." Jack closed the folder and placed it on Ed's desk. "What about the anchor that was found? Did they come up with any fingerprints?"

"Unfortunately, no. But there was a lot of rust that had started to flake off. It's not that surprising."

Jack expelled a small sigh. "So the question remains, how do we proceed from here?" Just then the door opened and Ryan walked in.

"Sorry I'm late," Ryan said, closing the door before taking a seat.

"You're not," Ed assured him. "Jack just beat you to the station. We were discussing what our next move on the case is going to be."

"I know we need to talk with Tim Camp and Kate Walter again," Ryan said.

"And Jim McCall," Ed stated as he pushed the manila folder in Ryan's direction.

Ryan had a curious look on his face as he opened the file. After a long pause, a soft whistle escaped from his lips. "McCall looks very close to our victim."

"Too close," Jack replied.

Ryan looked at him. "I watched him yesterday after we brought the body onboard the boat. I wanted to make sure that he didn't touch any potential evidence. There was absolutely no indication that he knew the woman. The man was totally stone–faced."

"Which could be a product of his military training," Ed suggested.

"Regardless of what it was, we need to interrogate him. I'd like a warrant to do a full search of the *Aphrodite,* as well as his residence," Jack said.

"I'll get the warrants," Ed promised. "Just let me know if you want to bring him in for formal questioning or make a surprise visit."

"The guy has the right to an attorney regardless. If we make an unannounced visit, at least we would be assured that he won't have additional time to clean up any possible evidence that may tie him to the murder."

"He had advanced warning early this morning when I spoke with him. If he has any common sense, he had to have realized that his association with Caryn Cooper and his reticence about making the fact known already placed a lot of attention on him," Ed pointed out.

"Have we been able to pull a background report on him?" Jack asked.

"It's being worked on as we speak. I'm hoping to have it on my desk by this evening. If not, first thing tomorrow."

"How about the background reports on Caryn's family?"

"They should be arriving sometime today."

Jack glanced at his watch. "How long do you think it will take for you to get the search warrants for McCall?" He wanted to get the searches under way as quickly as possible.

"Give me thirty minutes," Ed said, sensing Jack's impatience.

Ryan looked at Jack. "We'll need another search team to help us through this. We can jump sites easy enough but in order to get full coverage on the search we'll need assistance."

Ed's gaze encompassed both men. "Do you want to take the residence or the ship? I'll dispatch a team to the opposite location."

"We'll go to the house first," Jack said, wanting to see if it would reveal anything about McCall that wasn't noticeable on the yacht the previous evening.

"I'll put everything into place."

"While you're doing that, Ryan and I will head back to our desks and review the information we obtained last night. With a little luck, something will jump out at us that we may have missed."

"I'll let you know when we're ready to move," Ed promised.

"Sounds good." Jack replied, heading out.

At his desk, Jack reached for the phone.

"Who are you calling?" Ryan asked over his shoulder as he walked over to the coffeemaker.

"Ashley. I spoke to her earlier this morning after I arrived home and she made the connection between Jim McCall and Caryn Cooper. She promised that she would call some of her contacts down at the newspaper to see if she could get clarification on just how close the two of them were."

"How did she make the connection?"

"From an article that ran in the newspaper."

Ryan grunted, not surprised. "You know, there is something else that's very strange about this whole thing."

Jack held up on making the call. "What?"

"When we were talking to Sam and Joe Cooper last night, neither one of them mentioned anything about Jim McCall knowing Caryn."

"They probably didn't think anything about it. The man is Joe Cooper's employer."

"Yeah, but when the family was asked to identify the body, they were told how Caryn was found. Don't you think it was strange that Jim McCall's name wasn't brought up once?"

"I'm not sure that the name of the yacht was mentioned. We would have to ask Ed about that."

"Ask me what?" Ed questioned, walking out of his office and making his way over to Jack's desk.

"Were the Coopers aware that it was Jim McCall's yacht that we were on when Caryn's body was found?" Jack asked.

"No. It was immaterial."

"It's not now," Ryan said.

"No," Ed agreed. "Based on the news coverage, the family has to be aware of it at this point. It'll be interesting to see what their reaction will be to that fact."

"Ryan and I will speak to them again. We should be able to determine if there's something there that needs our attention."

Ed nodded. "The warrants will be ready in twenty minutes. You can pick them up on the way out."

Jack watched Ed walk inside his office, then looked at Ryan. "Let me call Ashley and then we'll get ready to head out."

"Sure."

Jack dialed his home number.

"Hi, babe. It's me," Jack greeted the moment he heard her voice. He heard John talking in the background and Ashley responding softly to him before she replied.

"Jack, I'm glad you called. I was just about to phone you."

"Is something wrong?"

"No. I wanted to let you know that I spoke with one of my contacts down at the newspaper."

"And?"

"And according to my source, Jim McCall, the *Aphrodite's* captain, and Caryn Cooper were friendly toward each other."

"How friendly?"

"They had met for dinner and drinks."

"Are you sure?"

"Yes. According to my source, Jim McCall liked

to eat at a restaurant by the marina. A waiter that works there stated that he had seen Jim and Caryn together at least twice."

Jack frowned at the news. "Was Caryn Cooper's husband Sam with them?"

"No. They were always alone."

## Chapter Eleven

Ryan noticed Jack's pensive silence as he ended the call. "What did Ashley say?"

Jack swiveled his chair around to face Ryan. "According to her source down at the newspaper, there definitely appeared more to Jim McCall and Caryn Cooper's relationship than just being acquaintances."

"That's makes it all the more important to get out to his house as soon as possible."

"I agree." Jack glanced at his watch and noted the time. "We should start heading over to pick up the warrants. They should be ready by the time we get there. Just give me a few minutes to go and let Ed know about what Ashley found out."

Jack was gone for only about five minutes before he returned. "Ed's going to see if he can corroborate the relationship between McCall and Cooper this afternoon. Between all three of us asking questions, we should be able to uncover something."

Ryan nodded and stood. "Then let's head out."

The sun was riding high in the sky when Jack and Ryan arrived at McCall's house, a modest high ranch-style home with a well-manicured lawn.

Jack parked by the curb and looked at the grounds. "The guy's house is immaculate," he said, noticing the freshly painted shutters and siding that gleamed in the afternoon sun. The lawn was lush and green, and the hedges were all trimmed and perfectly aligned. The flowers added bright splashes of color.

"With his military background, it doesn't surprise me that the outside of his home is kept so pristine," Ryan said, having found the man very regimented, very disciplined.

"Let's just hope that if he had anything to do with Caryn Cooper's murder, he wasn't as steadfast in cleaning up," Jack said, hearing the sounds of other vehicles approaching. He glanced in the rearview mirror. He noticed a couple of vans turning the corner, and he recognized them as belonging to the police department. "Here comes our reinforcements."

Ryan turned in his seat, catching sight of the police personnel. Two vans parked behind Jack's car by the curb, the last one blocked the driveway. He was about to turn back to face Jack, when out of the corner of his eye he saw McCall coming around the side of the house. "It looks like we have McCall's attention."

Jack frowned and followed Ryan's gaze. "It doesn't look like he's too happy to see us," he said as he noticed the man's facial expression and defensive stance.

"We can't blame him for that," Ryan replied, reaching for his door handle and exiting the car.

Jack joined Ryan, and they made their way to Mc-Call.

McCall had walked halfway down his driveway before he paused, his gaze on Jack and Ryan. "Detectives," he greeted formally, his face puzzled. His gaze flew briefly back to the police personnel that were exiting the vans. "What exactly is going on?"

Jack reached inside his suit jacket and pulled out the warrant. "Mr. McCall, we have a warrant to search your house."

McCall reached for the folded piece of paper and quickly flipped it open. "I don't understand."

"By now you've heard the identity of the body that was pulled from the water last night."

"Caryn Cooper?"

"From our understanding, you knew Mrs. Cooper," Ryan said.

"Her stepson worked for me. I knew her casually."

"Yet you didn't say you knew her when we pulled

her from the water. Didn't you recognize her?" Ryan asked.

Jack couldn't help but notice McCall suddenly stiffen, and got the distinct impression that he was buffering himself against an attack. "We have some questions that we need to ask you regarding your relationship with Caryn. Is there somewhere more private where we could talk?"

The pause that followed Jack's question was noticeable, but McCall quickly recovered his wits. "We can speak inside."

"Thank you. If you'll lead the way . . ." Jack turned back to the search team and gave the signal for them to begin.

McCall couldn't help but notice the gesture. "I take it that they'll try and keep the search as orderly as possible?"

"They will. And in all fairness, we should warn you. There's another search that's taking place on your yacht at this time."

Total silence filled the air.

"If you'd like to call your lawyer . . ."

McCall regained his equilibrium, and his eyes narrowed slightly. "Do I need a lawyer?"

"It's a matter of preference."

"Then I'll reserve judgment on that for now," McCall said, opening the front door to his home and stepping inside.

Jack and Ryan followed, noticing the renovation that was taking place inside. Two six-foot wooden ladders were on either side of the living room, and a heavy tarp that matched the one McCall had supplied when Caryn Cooper's body was found was spread over the furniture to protect it. Several cans of paint and supplies were lined up in the corner.

"It looks like you're in the middle of a home project," Ryan said, walking closer to the corner where the paint cans were lined up. A couple had already been pried open, the drips of white paint plastered to the side of the cans already dry. "When did you start this project?"

"A few days ago. Why?"

Ryan glanced at him. "No reason. Just curious." He looked at the other items on the floor. Beside the cans of paint, there was a box. Crouching down, he opened the flaps and looked inside. There was a lot of paraphernalia nestled inside, including several heavy sheets of plastic. But there was one thing in particular that caught his attention. About two feet of rope. Closing the flaps, he stood to his feet and motioned for one of the members of the search team to come over and collect the box.

McCall noticed the action. "Is that really necessary?" he asked as the box was removed and taken out to a van to be catalogued.

"It's procedure," Ryan assured him.

McCall didn't look entirely convinced by the explanation, but he didn't pursue it further. Instead, he motioned to the sofa that was covered by the tarp. "Take a seat."

Jack's gaze met Ryan's, and he caught Ryan's shake of his head. Knowing that Ryan had uncovered something, he said, "Actually, our search team needs to go through this room. Is there somewhere else we can talk?"

"I have an office downstairs."

"That would be fine," Jack replied, waiting as McCall took the lead.

The search team had firmly taken hold of the interior of the house as they made their way down the basement stairs off the kitchen, and Jack watched a couple of the investigators that had gone down to the basement before them search through the clothes hamper by the washer and dryer.

McCall also noticed their actions, and his hand tightened slightly on the stairway banister.

"We understand you were at a recent fund-raising luncheon with Caryn Cooper," Jack said casually, hoping to get the man's mind off the search. He knew the investigators were looking for any clues or evidence that Cooper had been in the home. Hair follicles or bloodstains attached to clothing or sheets might at least let them make a DNA connection in the case.

McCall glanced back at Jack, the look in his eyes telling Jack that he recognized the diversion tactic.

He didn't protest the search going on, but he also didn't respond immediately to Jack's comment. Instead, he led the way into a part of the basement that had been converted into a home office.

McCall waited until Jack and Ryan were seated in front of his desk before answering. "I was at the luncheon. I wanted to make a financial contribution to the cause. Fitness is something I've always been interested in, and it's been a huge part of my life."

"You're retired from the Navy?" Ryan questioned.

"For two years now. But to be honest, I miss being on the water."

"Is that why you purchased the yacht?" Jack asked.

"It's the main reason. The business I built keeps me close to the sea."

"And that leaves you enough time to pursue other interests?" Jack inquired.

"Enough. I usually rent out the yacht for private parties. Similar to the same kind of event we hosted for Police Captain Stall."

"How did you hear about the fitness committee?"

"A friend of mine, Peter Jenkins, told me about it. He knew that I liked to stay fit, and he thought I would be interested in what they were trying to do."

"And Caryn Cooper? How well did you know her?" Ryan questioned.

McCall shrugged. "As I said, just casually. We ran into each other once in a while on the streets. Her stepson works for me. It was natural that we'd be friendly."

"Yet you didn't recognize her when we pulled her body from the water," Ryan said.

"No. But in all fairness I was shocked. The last thing I expected to find floating in the water was a murder victim."

Jack sensed that McCall wouldn't be offering any further explanation, and he knew that it was entirely possible that the man was telling the truth. When it became apparent that he wasn't going to say anything else, Jack asked, "Did you ever see Caryn hanging out with anybody?"

"Her husband, Sam. Her stepson, Joe."

"How would you describe her relationship with her husband?"

"They appeared close."

"Last night when you were speaking to Captain Stall, you had mentioned that you thought Sam Cooper might be having second thoughts about his marriage."

McCall looked surprised. "I did?"

"Yes. You mentioned to him that Joe Cooper wasn't working last night, and that you made allowances due to tension in his household. At the time, you alluded that there might have been problems between Joe Cooper's father and his new stepmother."

When McCall didn't immediately respond to the

comment, Jack pressed, "There must have been something that gave you that impression."

McCall hesitated before saying, "There was."

"What was it?" Jack did not like the fact that the man wasn't talking freely. It made him doubt the validity of the observations.

"There were comments from Joe."

"Anything else?"

McCall leaned back in his chair. "A few times when I ran into Caryn, she seemed distracted. I finally asked her if everything was okay."

"What did she say?"

"She said that there was some tension between her and Sam." McCall fell silent with his thoughts.

"Whatever you tell us will be kept between the three of us. It goes no further unless it holds specific relevance to this investigation."

"I can only tell you what Caryn told me."

"Since Caryn can't speak on her own behalf, what you tell us may help find her murderer," Jack told him.

McCall nodded. "I don't know if you were aware of this or not, but Caryn was married before. Her first husband was Roger Camp."

"She's widowed," Ryan remarked.

"Yes. But she was very close to her first husband. They were practically inseparable."

"How do you know that?"

"Caryn told me. One night when we ran into each

other on the street, she seemed a little upset, distracted if you will. I suggested dinner. I thought it might help if she had an impartial person to talk to. Someone to just listen. She mentioned how much she missed Roger, and how jealous Sam seemed to be of her first marriage. At the time I didn't think much about it. A lot of men get jealous. It doesn't necessarily mean anything. But then she mentioned how Roger's son Tim was trying to establish some sort of relationship with her."

"Did she say if she knew what prompted Tim's actions?" Jack asked.

"She assumed that it was because he was never close to his father, and he was curious about what he was like."

"Why would you think that was just an assumption?"

"Because it was the terminology that Caryn used."

"What else did Caryn tell you?" Ryan asked.

McCall shrugged. "Not much. But I got the impression from Caryn that Sam resented her spending time with other people. On the night that we had dinner together, Caryn had told me that she and Sam had argued before she left the house. According to Caryn, Sam gave her an ultimatum. She either had to spend more time at home or their marriage was over."

## Chapter Twelve

Jack was careful not to show any reaction to the statement. He couldn't be sure if Jim McCall was actually stating a fact or trying to dig himself out of the hole that he found himself in. "What was Caryn's reaction to that?"

"Pretty much what you would expect. She didn't like it. I think it made her feel threatened."

"Did she say that?"

"What? That she was threatened?"

"Yes." Jack watched McCall's facial expression while he formulated an answer. He could tell that the man was being careful.

McCall was quiet for a long period. "Not in so many words."

"What were her words?"

"I don't remember exactly," McCall said.

Jack's eyes narrowed. It bothered him that the man was beating around the bush. "Then tell us what you recall."

"I can only give you my interpretation."

"Right now, your interpretation is all we have to go on."

When the man didn't answer, Jack prompted, "Mr. McCall?"

McCall expelled a harsh breath before he replied. "Caryn gave me the impression that she felt challenged."

"Challenged?" Ryan repeated.

"I think she wanted to prove something. She wanted to show Sam that he couldn't dictate her actions. That he had no control about who she allowed into her life."

"Including yourself," Jack deduced.

"That's one way of looking at it."

"Did you and Caryn go out on a regular basis without Sam?" Ryan asked.

"Not really. There was only one other instance when we had dinner together. And it was totally innocent. We were both dining alone at the same restaurant, so we decided to share a table."

"Did Caryn mention why she was dining alone?"

"She said Sam was away on business."

"How long ago was that?" Jack asked.

"A couple of weeks ago. But to be honest, it was a disaster."

"Why would you say that?" Ryan asked.

"Because her stepson Joe walked into the restaurant with his date. The tension that was in the air when Joe and Caryn acknowledged each other was thick enough to cut with a knife."

"What did Caryn do when she saw him?" Jack asked.

"She excused herself and went into the ladies' room. I saw Joe follow. I was a little concerned by the expression on his face, so I went after them."

Ryan frowned. "Did you think he would have hurt her?"

"Honestly, no." McCall's face became pensive as he thought about the events of that night. "Joe is a decent kid. He's young and impulsive, but I don't think he could deliberately hurt anyone. Physically at least."

The last part of the statement was not lost on Jack. "How about emotionally?"

"That he's capable of. I heard his comment to Caryn when he caught up with her. He accused her of cheating on his father."

"With you," Jack said.

"With me. Nothing could have been further from the truth, though. After I heard what Joe said, I interrupted their conversation. I made sure that he understood that we were only together by chance. That our friendship was just that. Friendship."

"And do you think he believed you?"

"Maybe not when he first saw us together at the restaurant, but after we discussed it with him I know he did."

"What makes you so sure of that?" Jack asked.

"I have a pretty good relationship with Joe. He's worked for me for quite a while. I spend a good deal of time with all my employees. I'm a firm believer in honesty and integrity, and I know the only true way to take the measure of a man's character is to get to know him. I believe that I had gained Joe's trust during his employment with me."

"In effect you're saying that you don't believe he had any option other than to take you at your word."

"My word and Caryn's. She was very sincere that night when she talked to him. She explained that she loved his father too much to do anything that would jeopardize their marriage."

"But Joe's loyalty would have been to his father."

"I know. And I'm quite sure Joe told Sam about seeing Caryn and I together. But I also know that Caryn would have made sure that Sam heard it from her before Joe could tell him."

"And you're basing that assumption on . . ."

"I'm basing it on the fact that she left shortly after

that. She told me that she needed to call Sam and do damage control. And before you ask, that was the way she phrased it."

"So she was worried," Ryan concluded.

"She was. But she had reason to be. By her own admission, she and Sam were having problems. The last thing she needed was for our dinner to be taken out of context."

Jack considered the information. "How long was it before you spoke to Caryn after that night?"

"It was a couple of days later. I ran into her at a diner on Main Street during lunch."

"Was she alone?"

"No, she was with Sam. Both of them were smiling, so I figured that they had worked through whatever problems they had."

"You didn't bring up the topic of your dinner together?" Ryan questioned curiously.

"No. I didn't think it was my place to. My relationship with Caryn was strictly platonic. I didn't want anybody to get any impressions otherwise. I figured the best thing I could do was to make sure that I didn't put myself in any more compromising positions."

"Just out of curiosity, how was Joe the next time you saw him?" Jack asked.

"He seemed fine. I had a cruise going out three days after that, and he called me to see if he could work it. He didn't mention the night at the restaurant, so I thought it best to follow suit."

Jack was quiet for a moment, wondering if McCall was going to expand on his comments. When it became obvious that he wasn't, Jack said, "You've been very helpful. We appreciate your cooperation."

McCall nodded. "Did you have any more questions?"

"I don't have any right now," Jack said before glancing at Ryan.

"I don't have anything else at the moment. But we may need to speak with you again," Ryan said.

"I'll help in any way I can."

Jack nodded and cast a quick glance at his watch before looking at Ryan. "We'd better go and see how the search is progressing."

"Do you know how much longer it will go on for?" McCall asked, his gaze shifting to the ceiling as he heard the heavy footsteps from the floor above.

"It'll probably be another couple of hours," Jack said, noticing the strain on the man's features. "We appreciate your cooperation. I know our being here is an inconvenience. We'll be out of here as quickly as possible."

## Chapter Thirteen

"**S**o, what was your impression?" Ryan asked Jack an hour later as they left the search that was still being conducted at McCall's residence.

"To be honest, I think the man is hiding something. Don't get me wrong, I think he did an admirable job in covering himself, but there's just something about his story that doesn't fit. He insists that he and Caryn were just casual acquaintances. But the photographic evidence that Ed came up with tells a different story."

"And then there's Ashley's comments."

"We can't ignore what her sources said," Jack agreed. "But the problem that we're facing is that there are too many other possible suspects for us to put McCall in the number one spot. We have Sam

Cooper, who by his own admission had a problem with jealousy where his wife was concerned. We have her stepson, Joe, who walked in on Caryn keeping company with McCall. If he already had doubts about the reason for Caryn's marriage to his father, it's possible that he didn't believe her when she told him that she loved Sam."

"But McCall said he thought that was smoothed over," Ryan reminded him.

"I know. But that could have only been an impression he got."

"Or wanted to get."

Jack grunted in agreement. "And we can't lose sight of the fact that Tim Camp may have had his own motive for wanting Caryn dead."

"I'm curious about what Tim Camp will say when we speak to him."

"I am too. Especially since his ex-girlfriend is the one that told us that she heard a splash coming from a cabin cruiser that was floating nearby on the night we found Caryn's body, and then he conveniently recalled the same thing."

"Let's head over to the dock and see if they uncovered anything from the yacht. Considering the fact that many of our suspects have had access to the vessel, there's a good chance that there's something there that could prove helpful with this investigation."

\* \* \*

Fifteen minutes later, Jack and Ryan were walking on board the *Aphrodite*. The entire vessel had been taped off as the police officers and crime technicians that had been dispatched to the site were removing evidence.

The police officer that was supervising the search was Paul Murphy, the same detective that Ed had assigned to help clear the deck of the *Aphrodite* the previous evening. Jack was glad that he was the one chosen. Murphy approached everything with a logical, no-nonsense approach.

"Did you find anything?" Jack asked, walking over to the man.

"The anchors used on the vessel are all accounted for, but there are a few things that might have some interest," Murphy responded.

"Such as?"

"In the excitement of last night, it appears as if someone left their duffle bag."

"No idea of who it belongs to?" Ryan questioned.

"We haven't searched it yet. We're dusting the area for prints now."

"Where was it found?" Jack asked.

"In the engine compartment."

"Not an obvious place to store something."

"No, I agree. Come on. I'll show you where it is."

Jack and Ryan followed Murphy to the compartment that held the engine. The area was small, barely big enough to hold a couple of people comfortably, and the crime scene technicians were diligently dusting all components for fingerprints.

Jack caught sight of the bag almost immediately, but he knew it was only because he was looking for it. It rested beside the main engine, the gray color of the fabric blending almost perfectly with the color of the engine. Reaching for a pair of latex gloves, he quickly donned them before he lowered himself into the compartment. Space was tight, and he was conscious of the fact that based on where the bag had been hidden, the person would have had to squeeze into the area. He couldn't help but be suspicious of just why the bag was placed in such an inconspicuous place.

He pulled the bag out from where it rested and glanced at the outside briefly, looking for anything that might help identify the owner. There were no tags, no markings of any sort. The one thing he noticed was that the zipper pull was missing. Reaching into his pocket for a pen, he wedged it into the small gap between the material and the zipper, and he carefully eased the zipper open. Though it was a long shot, he knew there was a possibility that Caryn's DNA might be present and he didn't want to disturb any physical evidence.

The zipper finally undone, Jack eased open the bag and looked at the contents. Inside he saw a couple of T-shirts and a towel. Carefully lifting one of the shirts out of the bag, he let it unfold, trying to gauge the size. It was a men's medium.

"Did you find anything, Jack?" Ryan asked.

Jack didn't immediately respond. Instead he removed a small black case that rested inside.

Ryan caught sight of the object. "That's a toiletry bag."

"How do you know?" Jack asked, opening the small pouch and confirming what Ryan had already guessed.

"Because Jane bought me one exactly like it for Christmas."

Jack grunted and placed the objects back in the bag so that the entire thing could be catalogued. Looking briefly around the area one final time, he made his way to the small entrance and levered himself out of the compartment.

"Somebody went through a lot of trouble to hide that bag," Jack said.

"There was no clue as to who?"

"No. It could belong to either a male or female. The contents were pretty generic."

"So the question is, why would someone go out of their way to hide it?"

Jack shrugged. "There was nothing valuable inside. Nothing that someone might be concerned about being stolen."

"Unless it held something else," Ryan suggested.

Jack's eyes narrowed. "You're thinking about the rope that could have possibly been used to tie Caryn Cooper's body to the anchor."

"It makes sense."

Jack expelled a harsh breath. "Yeah, it does. Maybe our next round of questions will reveal some answers."

## Chapter Fourteen

Later that afternoon, Jack was sitting at his desk, reviewing the preliminary background reports that had been delivered. Ed was nowhere in sight, and the desk sergeant didn't know when he was expected back. He had left the building over an hour ago, with no mention of where he was going.

Jack looked through the limited information of the reports, hoping that he would come across something, anything that would be a lead in the case.

As he sorted through the material, he thought about the day. After leaving McCall's yacht, he and Ryan had gone to the Cooper residence in the hope of speaking to Sam or Joe. But they had no luck. According to the housekeeper, both father and son had left, and she didn't know when they would be returning. The

102

woman didn't seem to have any idea of where the two men had gone, so Jack and Ryan thought it would be more productive to come back to the police station and check if any reports had come in. Though they didn't expect much as far as details yet, Jack was hoping that the information obtained would fill in a few pieces of the puzzle.

Ryan had gone to the break area as soon as they arrived back at the station, and Jack heard the sound of his footsteps as he returned. Glancing up, he reached for the can of soda that Ryan held out to him.

"Thanks," Jack said, popping the top and taking a long sip of the beverage.

Ryan took a seat, leaned back and stretched his legs out. "Is there anything specific in the reports that we need to follow up on?"

"There were a couple of calls to Caryn Cooper's cell phone the night she disappeared, but they originated from a pay phone."

"Any leads in voice mail messages or outgoing calls?"

"No. There's also no leads in Caryn's personal computer files based on the preliminary data."

"How about Joe Cooper's background report?"

"I don't see anything jumping out," Jack said. The information had the specifics regarding his date of birth, schools, employment records, driving history, and bank records, but it contained very little in the way of personal information relating to character reference. He handed Ryan the reports. "You can take a look and see if I missed anything."

Ryan opened it. "This is just basic information."

"It's stamped preliminary, so my guess is that more is coming."

Reaching for another file, Ryan reviewed the information obtained on Sam Cooper. "Sam Cooper's financial status is solid."

"So we can probably assume that he was being truthful when he told us about how he paid off Roger Camp's debt."

Ryan flipped a page. "Unfortunately, we weren't able to pull any information to trace the money transfer that paid off Roger Camp's creditors."

"True, but that may just mean that Camp's creditors weren't responsible for Caryn's death. If they weren't happy with the deal Sam offered to settle the debt, they would have continued to make contact. It doesn't take a genius to figure out that if Sam wanted to, he could have come up with additional money. They would have had to have known that too. I'm sure they did their own investigation on the man when they claimed the money Roger Camp owed them."

Ryan grunted and reached for another file. It was on Tim Camp. Sorting through the documents, he came across a copy of the custody agreement that had been filed in court from when Tim's mother and father separated. He took a moment to read through the details. "This confirms that Roger Camp gave up custody without a fight."

"I saw that."

"It says here that Roger Camp fought his first wife over alimony payments."

"But not child support. If you look at the document attached, the man wasn't late once with payment for Tim."

"No, that's true. But if Tim ever heard his parents arguing over money, depending on his age, he might not have realized that the man was supporting him."

Jack sat back in his chair. "So what's your theory? That Tim thought his father, Roger was neglecting him? I think that's a given."

Ryan glanced once more at the report. "Maybe his issues with his father weren't just because he wasn't around. Depending on how close Tim is to his mother, he could have taken Roger Camp's marriage to Caryn as a betrayal to them both."

"That would lead more weight to a motive for him to want to see her dead," Jack acknowledged.

"Jim McCall had mentioned that Caryn Cooper had told him that Tim Camp had been trying to find out information about his father. Maybe that's not really who he was interested in."

"You're thinking he was really interested in Caryn Cooper," Jack said, following Ryan's train of thought and finding it plausible. If Tim Camp felt that his father not only abandoned him, but also his mother, the target for his curiosity could have been Caryn. It's possible that he blamed her entirely for his father's actions. If he thought money was being withheld, it stood to reason that he would have assumed that his father's new wife was the cause.

"I don't think it would be a stretch to assume that Tim might have been trying to get to know Caryn so that he could become familiar with her habits and interests. Becoming friendly with her might have given him the information he needed about her so that he could manipulate circumstances. Maybe Caryn went to meet Tim in the early morning hours. If Tim made it seem urgent . . ."

Jack ran a hand absently across his chin while he contemplated Ryan's words. "His file lists both his home phone number and his cell phone number. It should be easy enough to cross-reference any calls he may have made to Caryn Cooper in the last forty-eight hours."

"If he made them from his phone."

"It'll give us a reference point," Jack said, swiveling his chair around slightly and reaching for the phone. Holding out a hand to Ryan, he took the folder and put in the request for Tim Camp's phone records.

"How long before we'll have it?" Ryan asked.

"A few hours at most."

Ryan nodded and motioned with his chin to the file that Jack hadn't looked at yet. "Who's that on?"

Jack opened the manila folder. "Kate Walter."

"Does it say anything?"

Jack sorted through the three pages. "She's attending school for her MBA." He reached for the file he had looked at on Joe Cooper, and opening it, he compared some information.

"Do you see something?"

"She's attending the same university that Joe Cooper is."

"So she has ties to both Tim Camp and Joe Cooper outside of work."

"Yeah, she does. They graduated high school and received their undergraduate college degrees at the same time," Jack revealed.

Ryan tapped his fingers on his desk. "It will be interesting to find out how well Joe Cooper and Kate Walter know each other. We know she had a past relationship with Tim Camp, but nobody mentioned anything about Joe."

"Attending the same schools, maybe even the same classes, and working together on board McCall's boat would indicate that they're more than just casual acquaintances."

"A confirmation of that would enable us to determine if there's anything else between them."

Jack glanced at his watch. "Yeah, it would. Do you want to head out now to talk to her? It's early enough."

"We don't have a warrant to search her house."

"We might not need one. It all depends on what she says or doesn't say."

"Last night she wasn't that cooperative," Ryan reminded him.

"I know. But maybe she will be today, especially if no other people are around."

"What about Ed?"

"What about him? He's not here at the moment, and I'd really like to cover as many bases as possible today and try and get a handle on this investigation. If we can speak to Kate Walter, we might be able to get some answers on not only her, but also on Tim Camp, Joe Cooper, and Jim McCall."

Ryan gave a slight shrug. "I'm game."

"Good," Jack said, rising from his desk. "Let me just run over to the lab. They should be bringing in the evidence from McCall's residence and ship. I'll ask that they put a rush on the preliminary findings and report back to us as quickly as possible."

"While you're doing that, I'll call Jane and let her know that I'll be working late tonight."

## Chapter Fifteen

Thirty minutes later, Jack parked his car by the wooden stockade that separated Kate Walter's apartment complex from the residential area it bordered. The two-story brick building was old and in need of repair. Aged, white paint had peeled from the wooden doors that faced the parking area, and shrubs that were slowly dying lined the cracked cement walkway that led to the doorways.

Shutting off the engine, Jack noticed that several of the screens were missing from the windows, many of which were an open invitation to anybody. The sounds of people talking mingled with loud music, and the heavy noise filtered into the parking area, causing Jack to inwardly cringe. "Our report stated that Kate Walter was attending school for her MBA.

I can't imagine that she gets much studying done if she has to contend with this noise."

"It doesn't look like the best place for a young woman to be living alone."

"No, it doesn't. But maybe she doesn't have the finances for someplace better. Graduate school doesn't come cheap."

"Ain't that the truth."

Jack opened his car door and stepped onto the worn blacktop. He motioned to the open window that seemed to be supplying some of the music. "That's her apartment. I would say she has to be home. Let's see if she'll talk."

The sound of rock music became louder as Jack and Ryan neared the wood panel and, pausing by the doorway, Jack knocked three times.

The volume was immediately lowered, and the distinct sounds of footsteps could be heard as someone approached the door. The vertical blinds were shifted and Walter peered outside.

Jack caught sight of her startled expression. "Ms. Walter, it's Detective Reeves and Detective Parks. We'd like to talk to you."

There was a slight pause before the blinds were repositioned and the door was opened.

"Detectives. I didn't expect to see you," Walter said, running her hand restlessly through her hair that was damp from a recent shower.

Jack didn't miss the gesture that was reminiscent

of the nervous habit she had displayed the previous evening. He also couldn't help but notice that she didn't invite them in.

"I apologize if this is bad timing, but we were wondering if we could speak with you," Jack said.

Walter's eyes met his. "I have to meet someone in an hour."

"We'll try to keep it brief." Jack got the impression that she was trying to think of an excuse not to talk to them.

When she still hesitated, Jack knew his impression was correct. He couldn't help but wonder exactly what it was that made the woman so leery about talking to the police. They had done nothing to intimidate her, nothing that should have threatened her. "Ms. Walter?"

Walter held his gaze for a long moment before slowing nodding. She stepped back from the doorway to let them into her apartment. "Okay."

"Thank you." Jack immediately took the opportunity to look around. Though they didn't have a search warrant, Jack knew that you could often pick up clues about a person's personality and lifestyle just by the possessions they kept. Walter's living room said a lot, mainly that she lived simply, and without luxuries. Though summer was in full swing, there was no air conditioner unit or fan to cool the interior. And with the exception of a long sofa, a chair, and television, the rest of the items in the room were exercise equipment. A treadmill, exercise bike, and stair climber all took up residence against a wall.

"You work out," Jack said.

"Yes," she answered, soft and cautious.

Jack realized that though she had allowed them access to her home, she wasn't willingly going to divulge anything. He knew he needed to get her to relax. "Do you ever work out at a gym? Or are your activities normally confined to the home?"

"Usually at the house, but I also jog."

"So I guess you were familiar with the project that Caryn Cooper was involved in regarding the new gym for the underprivileged."

"Yes."

"Were you involved?"

"Involved?"

"With the project," Jack supplied.

Walter gave a slight shrug. "I guess you could say that."

Jack repressed a sigh at the woman's evasion and kept his facial expression neutral. "In what capacity?"

"I donated some of my home gym equipment that I haven't used in a while."

"That was generous of you."

Walter shrugged off the compliment. "It was nothing. I'm always trying out new things. The latest fads. Most of which I don't stay with. At least by donating the items, I didn't feel as though the money spent on them was being thrown away." She paused for a long moment. "I was shocked to hear that the woman found last night at Captain Stall's party was Caryn."

"Who told you?" Jack asked.

"Joe Cooper. We're actually pretty good friends. We grew up together and hung out with the same crowd in high school. He's the person I'm meeting tonight."

Jack was curious about that. "I know you had said that you don't have a lot of time, and I promised to keep this brief, but would it be okay if we sat down?"

She looked surprised by the request, as if she hadn't realized that they were standing in the entranceway of her apartment. "Of course. Please have a seat."

Jack and Ryan waited until she took a seat in a chair before they sat down on the sofa.

Jack watched her carefully. "Ms. Walter, I'd like to be honest with you. The reason we're here to talk to you today is because of your relationship with Joe Cooper. We knew before coming here that you both attended the same schools. We were hoping that you would help us fill in some blanks regarding the Cooper family so that we can find out who's responsible for killing Caryn Cooper."

"What did you want to know specifically?"

"Well to start, how is Joe handling his stepmother's death?"

"It's hard on him. It's hard on the whole family. His father, Sam, especially. He and Caryn had a special relationship."

"What do you mean by special?"

"Just that they seemed very close."

"Did you spend a lot of time with them?"

Walter shook her head. "Not really. But the times I was with Joe at the house and they were there, Sam and Caryn were always laughing about something."

"So from outward appearances, you wouldn't think that they were experiencing any problems," Jack said, recalling Jim McCall's words about the Coopers' relationship.

"Not that I could tell."

"How long ago did you donate the exercise equipment to the fitness committee?"

"It was only a couple of months ago. Shortly after I learned that they were looking for donations. As I said, I'm always trying something different. Weight training, a rower. I keep trying things until I find something that holds my interest. So, I usually have an accumulation of things gathering dust. When I learned that they were looking for things of that nature, I thought it would be a good opportunity to clean house and maybe do someone some good."

"Mrs. Cooper must have been pleased with your donation," Ryan said.

"I hope she was. I would hate for her to think that I gave Joe the stuff just to get it out of my way."

"She never acknowledged your donation?" Jack asked.

"No. To be honest, I'm not even sure that Joe told her that I was the one who made it. He never mentioned it after the night I gave him the equipment, and neither did Caryn."

"Is there any reason why you think Joe wouldn't have mentioned the donation to Caryn?"

"No. It's just that the topic was never brought up by either of them again. And the items weren't valuable enough to ask for any type of receipt for tax purposes."

"You said you and Joe were good friends," Jack said, going back to her original statement.

"I consider Joe a great friend."

"When was the last time you saw him?"

"The night before last," she said, corroborating what Joe had told them.

"That was the night that Caryn Cooper went missing," Ryan stated.

"Yes."

"What time did you see him?" Jack asked, keeping his tone neutral. She was talking willingly, which was something that she didn't do the previous night.

"Around ten. We went to The Sand Pit," she said.

"Who was there?"

"Actually, most of the people we work with on the *Aphrodite*."

"Was Jim McCall there?"

She gave a small laugh. "No. Clubbing has never been Jim's thing. He's too structured for that."

"How about Tim Camp?" Ryan questioned.

"Tim was there," she admitted. "He arrived late though."

"How late?"

"About midnight."

"Just out of curiosity, did Tim and Joe get along?" Jack asked.

Walter thought about the question. "There's always been a little bit of tension between the two of them."

"How long have they known each other?"

"Since high school."

"Would you consider them friends?"

"Not close friends. But they were both on the weightlifting team in high school. They had mutual friends that forced them to socialize together."

"You had mentioned that Tim had arrived at the club around midnight. What time did everybody stay until?"

"Tim and I left around two in the morning."

"And what about Joe? What time did he leave?"

"He left shortly after Tim arrived. He said he had some things to take care of."

"Can you estimate the time that he left?" Ryan asked.

"Maybe a half hour after Tim arrived. Twelve-thirty or so."

"Did he say what he had to take care of?"

"No. He just said that he needed to take care of something for Caryn. I assumed it had something to do with the fitness committee."

"The hour was kind of late for him to be working on something relating to that project," Jack pointed out.

"It was. But Joe often did things at night. To be honest, I didn't give his comment a second thought."

"What do you mean that he did things at night?" Ryan questioned.

"The cruises on the *Aphrodite* usually last until the early morning hours. It's not unusual for us to be docking at two in the morning. It usually takes another hour or two with everybody pitching in to clear off the ship."

"So basically what you're saying is that his internal clock doesn't wind down at midnight. He still has energy to spare."

"That's the best way of putting it."

"Did you ask Joe specifically what he was doing that night?" Jack asked.

"No."

"Then how did you come to the conclusion that he was doing something for Caryn?"

"Because she called him on his cell phone right before he left."

## Chapter Sixteen

A short while later, Jack and Ryan were on their way back to the police station. They wanted to check with the lab regarding the evidence that had been uncovered at Jim McCall's, and they were hoping that Ed would be back so that they could discuss the day's events.

"So what did you think of Kate Walter's comments?" Ryan asked, reaching out to adjust the flow of cool air from the vent on the dashboard.

"She seemed sincere in her admiration for the Coopers," Jack said, reaching out to adjust his own air vent. He was still feeling the effects of the lack of air conditioning in Walter's apartment.

"Yeah, she did. I don't doubt that she and Joe

Cooper are friends with each other. She seemed genuinely concerned about the family."

"But her take on the family is slightly different than Jim McCall's," Jack pointed out. "Kate Walter saw them as loving and affectionate. McCall seemed just as certain that the couple was experiencing problems. And I have to say that based on Sam Cooper's comments on jealousy, I'm inclined to believe that McCall had the more accurate portrayal of what was really going on between Caryn and Sam Cooper."

"And if that's the case, we'll have to determine who called Joe on the night Caryn disappeared. Was it Sam or Caryn?"

"You think the call that Joe received on his cell phone could have been from his father?" Jack asked.

"It's definitely a possibility. The relationship between the two of them seemed fairly close. It's not a stretch to think that Joe would cover for something his father did."

"No, it's not," Jack agreed, just as Ryan's cell phone rang.

"Parks."

"Ryan, this is Ed. Are you with Jack?"

"Yeah. Why?"

"Where are you?"

"On the way back to the station. We stopped by earlier but you were gone. We just got through paying a visit to Kate Walter."

"Well, get yourselves down to the beach in Carrier Park. I can't be certain until testing is completed, but I'm pretty sure that evidence from Caryn Cooper's murder just surfaced."

"We'll be right there," Ryan assured him before disconnecting the call.

"Was that Ed?"

"Yeah."

"What did he say?" Jack asked.

"He's at Carrier Park. Something washed ashore that he believes may be related to the Cooper murder."

"Did he say what?"

"No. He just asked that we meet him there."

"We're only about fifteen minutes away." Jack performed a sharp u-turn and headed to the park.

The parking lot of Carrier Park had already been secured by police personnel when Jack reached the chainlink fence that protected the area. Stopping the car briefly to flash his badge to one of the officers guarding the gate, he drove into the lot and parked by the entrance.

Jack took in the scene. Though dusk was just beginning to fall, the hot summer day had people out in droves, enjoying the beach that the park was known for. From his vantage point, Jack could see that the police were still trying to get people to vacate the area. The white gazebo where summer concerts were held had stragglers hanging around watching the police activity, and officers were ushering bystanders off the walking paths by the picnic areas on a bluff. The scenic park was popular with both locals and tourists alike, and it looked like the attendance that day was a record high.

Ryan looked at the activity. "The crowd doesn't look like it's dispersing."

"No, it doesn't." Jack caught sight of a couple of news crews already doing live feed of the proceedings, and he realized that the crowd that was gathered outside the fence would only increase as people watched the broadcast. His eyes scanned the inside of the park. "I don't see Ed anywhere. Let's head on down to the water's edge and see if he's there."

Ryan followed Jack through the gated entrance and down the footpath that led to the concession stand a short distance from the water. The police presence was heavier as they neared Long Island Sound, but they were able to locate Ed almost immediately.

Ed was down on one knee, talking to a small dark-headed boy that couldn't have been more than seven or eight. The sunburn and swimming shorts on the child suggested the boy had been playing in the water, and the way Ed was talking to him was an indication that he must have had something to do with the evidence being uncovered. A couple was standing protectively off to the side watching the child carefully.

Ed looked up as they approached. "I'm glad you

two are here," he said, rising to his feet and turning toward the adults. "This is Russ and Mary Taylor. Mr. and Mrs. Taylor, this is Detective Reeves and Detective Parks."

Jack immediately stepped forward to greet them. He then glanced down at the boy who was looking up at him curiously. He crouched down to make eye contact. "Hi," he said.

Ed laid a light hand on the boy's shoulder. "This is Michael. The Taylors' son. He was in the water playing when he found a length of rope."

Jack nodded, not needing Ed to fill in any more blanks at the moment. He knew that Ed believed that the rope found was evidence in Caryn Cooper's murder.

"So you found the rope?" Jack asked gently. He sensed that Michael was slightly disconcerted, though the child seemed to have a natural curiosity about the police proceedings.

Michael nodded. "It was in the water."

"Was it floating?"

"No. It was on my foot. I thought it was a snake."

"A snake. That must have been scary."

"It was. I called my dad," he said, looking over to the man that held the title.

Jack glanced briefly at Russ Taylor. He looked back to Michael. "Then what happened?"

"My dad came. He reached down and picked up the rope. But it wouldn't come out of the water."

Jack looked at Michael's father curiously.

The man met his gaze. "The rope wouldn't come out of the water because it was tied to something."

"What?" Jack asked.

"Part of a heavy gauge steel chain."

Jack scanned the area until he saw the object in question. The chain was thick and it looked like it could be used in conjunction with a ship's anchor. The large S-style hook that was attached to the end was proof that it had become disengaged from an object. Jack's eyes met Ryan's in a moment of silent communication.

Ryan stepped forward to inspect the items. A crime scene investigator had already catalogued and tagged the items and Ryan reached for a pair of latex gloves. After he examined the chain, he studied the rope that was tied to it through one of the links. He recognized immediately that the rope was very similar to the one they had uncovered at Jim McCall's residence that day.

Ryan glanced at Russ Taylor. "Are you the one who contacted the police?"

"No, I am," said a man who stepped out of the crowd. It was Tim Camp.

## Chapter Seventeen

"You did," Jack said, his words a comment and not a question, as he tried to reconcile the evidence found on the beach and Tim Camp's presence at the same location.

Camp stepped forward and held out a hand to Michael. The child immediately ran over to him. "Michael's my cousin. His father's my uncle on my mother's side."

Jack's gaze went to Russ Taylor, but the man's attention was focused on his son.

"Michael, why don't you and your mother start to head over to the car," Russ directed.

Michael looked up at his father before he nodded. With a final glance in Jack's and Ryan's direction, he took his mother's hand and he let her lead him away.

Camp waited until the child was out of earshot before he spoke. "When Russ pulled the rope out of the water and we realized it was attached to something, our curiosity got the better of us. I borrowed Michael's swim mask and dove under the surface. The chain was imbedded in the sand. Based on everything that's happened, and the news report of an anchor being found that's been linked to Caryn Cooper's murder, I thought it best to call the police and report it."

"We're glad you did," Jack said.

"I was shocked to hear that the woman found last night was Caryn," Camp admitted.

There was a lot of emotion in the single statement, and Jack took a few moments to study Camp. There was a sense of desolation in Camp's tone of voice, and his body language suggested he was having a hard time reconciling the woman's death. The strain that was evident on the man's features and his bloodshot eyes were indications that there was some type of relationship between Camp and Cooper.

"Were you close to Caryn?" Jack asked.

Camp ran a restless hand through his short brown hair, causing the strands to stand on end. "Not very. Not as close as I would have liked to be," he replied, his voice choking.

Russ Taylor laid a hand on Camp's shoulder and addressed Jack. "My wife and I are the ones who asked Tim to join us today. Tim told us everything that had happened last night, and we knew he was upset. We thought it would do him good to get out of the house for a while."

"We understand." Jack looked at Camp curiously. "Are you up to answering some questions?"

"If I can."

Jack glanced at Taylor then back at Camp. "Maybe it would be best if we did this one on one."

Camp shook his head. "I'd like my uncle to stay if it's all right with you."

Jack glanced briefly at Ryan and Ed before nodding. "If that's what you'd prefer."

"It is."

Jack nodded. "Can I ask how far out in the water you were today when Michael discovered the rope?"

"About twenty feet from shore. I took Michael out on a raft and he fell off before I could catch him," Camp replied.

"He swims?" Jack asked.

"Like a fish," Taylor responded. "But he got understandably nervous when the rope twisted around his leg."

Jack nodded slightly before turning his attention back to Camp. "I understand you've kept in touch with Caryn after your father passed away."

"Yes. I wanted to know about my father. She was married to him before she met Sam Cooper."

"We know. How did you find out that the woman found was Caryn Cooper?"

"From the news."

"Joe Cooper didn't call you?"

"Why would he?"

"I understand that you two sometimes hung out together," Jack replied, watching him closely.

Camp stilled at the comment. "Kate Walter told you that."

"Yes, but Joe Cooper also mentioned it."

"You went to talk to Kate today?"

"We had some additional questions for her."

"I'm surprised that Kate would talk to you."

"Why?" Ed asked.

Camp looked at his uncle briefly. "She's not comfortable speaking with the police."

Jack kept his expression neutral. "Any idea why?"

Camp shrugged. "She doesn't trust them. She was once accused of something she didn't do, and I think the ordeal was a bit much for her."

"She was questioned by the authorities?" Jack asked, knowing that the information wasn't noted in her background check.

"It never got that far."

"What do you mean?"

Camp made eye contact with his uncle once again, and Jack got the impression that there was some type of communication taking place.

"Tim?" Jack prompted.

Taylor inclined his head to Tim. "Tell them."

Camp was quiet for a moment longer. "Caryn accused Kate of stealing some jewelry from their house."

"Caryn Cooper?" Jack asked.

"Yes. Except it wasn't true," Camp said. "If it was, Caryn would have called the police instead of confronting Kate directly."

"Do you know what happened? What led to the accusation being made?"

Camp shrugged. "Not really. All I know is that some jewelry disappeared, and because Kate was spending a lot of time at the house with Joe, she seemed to get the blame."

"Do you know if the jewelry ever surfaced?" Ryan asked.

"I'm not sure. I didn't think it was my place to ask. Quite frankly, I didn't really want to get involved. I listened while Kate vented, but I never brought up the topic with either Kate or the Coopers. Kate was a little upset over that. She thought I should have stood up for her because of our past. To be honest, she's been a little cold to me since then. She never seemed to understand that I wasn't about to get in the middle of anything. It wasn't my place to. Our relationship had already ended when the incident occurred."

"She didn't seem cold last night," Jack said, watching Camp carefully as he made the statement, looking for some sort of reaction.

Camp sighed and ran a hand wearily across the back of his neck. "She was looking for support last night. If I wasn't there, she would have turned to someone else."

"Do you believe that incident is why she seemed so reluctant to talk to us last night?" Ryan asked.

"I know it was. The accusation from Caryn really shook her, especially since Caryn threatened to report it to the police."

"Was that what she was whispering to you about when people were disembarking from the yacht?" Jack asked.

"Yes," Camp confirmed, not bothered or surprised by the fact that they had been observed.

Jack contemplated the information. Their conversation with Camp wasn't really answering any questions. Instead it seemed to put more suspicion on other people. "How would you classify your relationship with Joe Cooper?" he asked curiously.

Camp took his time in answering. "Joe and I weren't exactly what you would call friends."

"What were you?"

Camp shrugged. "To be honest, I'm not sure. Friendly acquaintances, maybe."

"So you didn't find it strange that nobody from the Cooper family called you and told you about Caryn's death?" Ryan asked.

"Not really. Don't get me wrong. It would have been nice if they had thought enough about me to let me know. But I understand why they didn't. Understandably, they're upset."

"But you're not?" Jack asked.

"I wouldn't say that."

"What would you say?"

"I'm naturally disturbed by the news. Caryn and I weren't that close, but when I wanted to know things about my father she was kind enough to talk to me."

"You never had a relationship with your biological father?"

"No. I can't say that it was ever something he desired. I think he was more interested in starting a new life." Some of the bitterness Camp felt over the situation leaked into his words.

"Did you know Caryn when she had been married to your father?" Ryan asked.

"I met her. I can't really say that I knew her all that well. Other than spending the occasional evening with them, my contact was pretty limited."

"And how did that make you feel?"

"I didn't want to see anybody dead if that's what you're getting at," Camp replied, his body tensing in anticipation at the next question.

"Nobody's suggesting that you did," Jack assured him, realizing that the questioning was beginning to take a toll on him. "We're just trying to get some answers so that we can make sense of everything. We need all the help we can get if we're going to find Caryn's murderer."

"Of course. I apologize if I sounded a little defensive."

"Don't worry about it," Jack told him, pausing for a moment. "When was the last time you saw Caryn?"

"It was the day before she disappeared."

"Where did you see her?"

"At a fast food restaurant in town. I didn't actually talk to her. She was with somebody and I didn't want to interrupt."

"Do you know who she was with?"

"Jim McCall."

Ed stepped forward. "What were they doing?"

"I'm not really sure. Like I said, I didn't want to interrupt their conversation. It looked pretty involved."

"Was anybody else present?" Jack asked.

"No," Camp replied, falling silent suddenly.

"What are you remembering, Tim?"

His eyes met Jack's. "I can't be certain, but I think I may have seen Sam Cooper's car in the parking lot."

"Maybe Caryn took the car," Jack suggested.

"No. The car I saw was a sports car. I know for a fact that it had a stick shift. I noticed it when I walked by. Caryn couldn't drive a stick shift."

"How do you know that?"

"Because Joe was joking about it one night. His father had bought the car for Caryn as a birthday present, and according to Joe, Caryn had accused Sam of actually buying the car for himself since she couldn't drive it."

"Do you think that Caryn knew that the car was in the parking lot?"

"I doubt it. The car was parked on the opposite side of the restaurant from where Caryn and Jim were sitting."

"You said you recognized the car, but did you see anybody in it?" Ryan pressed.

Camp slowly shook his head. "No. I suppose anybody could have been driving it. Anybody but Caryn that is."

"Are you sure that the car belonged to the Coopers?" Jack asked.

"Not one hundred percent, but fairly sure," Camp said with a shrug.

"Do you know if Joe Cooper can drive a stick shift?"

"I know he can. His first car had a stick shift."

Jack made a mental note of the fact. "Can you think of anything else about the day that you saw Caryn? Anything that sticks out in your mind?"

"No. That's pretty much it." Camp watched as a technician lifted the chain and the rope, and placed it in evidence. "I wish I could tell you something else that would help, but to be honest I really don't recall much right now."

"You've been very helpful. If you can think of anything else, would you call us? I believe you have the number."

Camp nodded. "It was given to me by the officer

who interviewed me last night." He looked at his uncle. "Let's go find Michael and Mary."

Jack waited until the men were out of sight before he addressed Ryan and Ed. "I don't like the fact that Tim admitted to seeing McCall with Caryn the other day. Or that he thinks he recognized one of the Coopers' cars in the parking lot of the restaurant."

"No, that is suspicious," Ed agreed. "But the question is, how do we prove who was in the car? If it did belong to the Coopers, it could have been Joe or Sam."

"There's a chance that both of them could have had something to do with Caryn's death," Ryan said.

"Yeah, there is. But there's also a chance that Tim might have fabricated some of the information he told us."

"There's always that chance, but I can tell you one thing," Ryan said.

"What?" Ed asked.

"I'm almost a hundred percent sure that the chain and rope found had to do with Caryn's murder."

"How can you be so sure?" Jack asked, knowing that the current would have had to be strong to carry the weight of the chain.

"Because there's a few strands of hair imbedded in the rope's fibers. I didn't want to mention it in front of Tim and his uncle, but my guess is that the strands will be a match for Caryn Cooper's."

## Chapter Eighteen

The following morning, Jack met Ryan and Ed at a nearby restaurant for breakfast so that they could discuss the case. They were seated at a far corner of the restaurant, away from prying eyes and ears. Most of the patrons of the diner were on their way to work, and the hustle and bustle of the waitresses as they seated people and cleared tables ensured that nobody would be focused on their meeting. The dining room was just emptying from the morning rush when the waitress came by to remove their plates and refill their coffee cups.

"I appreciate you two meeting me here," Ed said as he stirred a packet of artificial sweetener into his coffee. "When I got the call from the lab this morning regarding the rope found at Carrier Park, I wanted to get a running start on this day. I thought this was the most expedient way for us to do that."

"What did they find?" Ryan asked.

"You were right about the strands of hair embedded in the fibers matching Caryn Cooper."

"Which is what we expected," Ryan said. "What about the rope from Jim McCall's house? Did anything show?"

"There's no physical evidence that we can tie to Caryn. The rope is the same thickness and type as the one found at the park, but it's also common."

Ryan lifted an eyebrow and took a sip of his coffee. "So, the first thing we have to do is review what we have so far on the people we targeted as possible suspects."

"I agree. Let's start with Sam Cooper," Ed replied.

Ryan cradled his coffee cup between his hands. "We know that Sam and Caryn are suspected of having marital problems."

"Jealousy in itself isn't a motive for murder," Ed reminded him.

"No. But if Sam Cooper actually caught his wife with another man, if he suspected her of infidelity, that might have been enough to send him over the edge," Jack replied.

"Do you think Tim Camp actually saw one of the Coopers' vehicles outside the restaurant?" Ed asked.

"I don't think it's something we can discount. But we don't know if it was Sam Cooper in the vehicle or if it was Joe Cooper," Ryan said.

"McCall said something when we were speaking with him yesterday that might somehow be connected to all of this," Jack recalled.

"What?" Ed asked.

"We questioned him on how often he saw Caryn socially. He claimed he only saw her twice. He didn't mention the incident at the fast food restaurant on the day before she disappeared."

"Do you think he didn't say anything about it because it was just a chance meeting?" Ed asked.

Jack shrugged. "That remains to be seen. It's possible. But he admitted that during one of the times that he dined with Kate, Joe had walked into the restaurant. According to McCall, Joe didn't handle finding them together well. He had to assure Joe that the meeting was innocent. McCall stated he was under the impression that the situation was defused by the time everybody left, but based on the information that's surfacing, there's the chance that Joe suspected Caryn of carrying on with Jim McCall."

"Meaning that if Tim actually saw a car belonging to the Coopers outside the restaurant the other day, Joe Cooper could have been the one driving it," Ed deduced.

"And if that's the case, there are two possibilities about what happened. Either Joe accidentally stumbled upon them at the restaurant and he hung around after seeing them together, or he followed them. Maybe Joe suspected that Caryn and Jim were seeing each other. If he did, he would probably want some kind of confirmation before he reported back to his father," Jack said.

"Which doesn't exactly give us any answers as to who killed Caryn Cooper," Ed said. "Do you think there's a chance that Joe was responsible for Caryn's murder?"

"It's a possibility," Ryan confirmed. "When we spoke with Kate Walter yesterday, she admitted to having been out with Joe Cooper on the night that Caryn disappeared."

"So?" Ed prompted.

"She said that Joe left after speaking with Caryn on the phone."

"Did she have a time?"

"Around twelve-thirty in the morning. We ran a trace on his phone records. A call from the Cooper household was placed to Joe's cell phone. We just don't know if Caryn made the call or if Joe's father Sam did. Jack and I went to their house to talk to them after speaking with McCall yesterday, but neither one of them were around, and the housekeeper didn't know where they had disappeared to," Ryan said.

"So we still need answers from them," Ed said, taking a sip of his rapidly cooling coffee. "What was

Jim McCall's behavior like when you showed up at his house?"

"I would say he was shocked," Jack replied.

"Leery," Ryan added.

Ed grunted. "Other than the fact that the man had a relationship with Caryn Cooper that at least on the surface seems more than platonic, we don't have any evidence except circumstantial that can possibly tie him to her murder. No motive has presented itself. Even if he was having an affair with her, nobody heard them arguing over anything," he said. "You didn't find anything else at his house or on the yacht?"

"There was a duffle bag that we found in an engine room on the yacht. We can't be sure if there's any tie to it and the murder," Jack said.

Ed frowned. "What did it contain?"

"A change of clothes, nothing valuable. It's really not what it contained that was so suspicious, but rather the location of where it was stored."

"It's in evidence now?"

"Yeah. We'll have to see if we can pick up any fingerprints," Jack said, his voice trailing off as his full attention focused on the glass door that led into the restaurant.

Ryan noticed Jack's preoccupation and swiveled in his seat to see what Jack was looking at. "Joe Cooper is here."

Ed turned. "He looks like he's on his way to the

gym to work out," he said, noticing the man's gym shorts and T-shirt.

Jack shifted his gaze to Ed. "He's carrying the same type of duffle bag that was found on McCall's yacht."

## Chapter Nineteen

Jack got up from the table and walked over to Joe Cooper. The man had just put his wallet away after paying for a cup of coffee to go, and had not realized that Jack was standing behind him.

"Mr. Cooper," Jack said.

Cooper quickly turned. "Detective Reeves," he greeted, surprised to see him. His eyes immediately searched the restaurant until he noticed Ryan and Ed sitting at a table, their attention focused entirely on him. He turned back to Jack, a curious look on his face. "Have you found out anything about Caryn's murder?"

Jack didn't answer Cooper's question. He was too conscious of the attention from the woman who stood behind the cash register. "Do you have a moment?"

"If it's about Caryn, I'll make the time."

"I'd appreciate that. Why don't we go back to the table. I know Captain Stall and Detective Parks would like to be part of this conversation."

"Sure," Cooper said, picking up his Styrofoam cup.

Jack led the way back to the table. He was aware of the few patrons of the restaurant following their progress, people that had paid no attention to Ryan, Ed, and himself prior to Cooper entering the restaurant. The fact that they were suddenly so interested spoke volumes for the fact that most of them knew that Cooper's stepmother had been killed, something that didn't surprise him. The morning edition of the newspaper had Caryn's picture plastered on the front page, along with a small photograph of the Cooper family at a Memorial Day barbecue. Cooper was easily recognizable from the photo.

Jack gestured to an empty chair at the table. "Please, have a seat."

Cooper sat down, nodding greetings to Ryan and Ed. Reaching for the plastic cover on his coffee, he lifted the lid and took a sip. "So, tell me, what have you found out regarding Caryn?"

Jack resumed his own seat before saying, "We'll get to that in a minute. Right now, can you tell us where you and your father were yesterday?"

Joe seemed surprised by the question. "One of the principals on the fitness committee for the new gym invited us to his house for the day. I'm afraid once the story broke that Caryn had been murdered, the press was all over our own property."

"Whose house were you at?" Ryan asked.

"Peter Jenkins."

Jack recognized the name as the same person who Jim McCall had stated convinced him to go to the fund-raising luncheon. He was suddenly curious about the man's connection to the suspects in the case. He knew it was somebody that he and Ryan would be checking out that afternoon.

"What's the man's relationship to you and your father?" Jack asked.

"He's a friend. He knew that we would be bombarded with reporters, and he thought it would be easier for us if we left the house for a while."

"Did you go anywhere other than his house?" Ryan asked.

"We went to the construction site for the new gym. Peter Jenkins set up an impromptu memorial service for Caryn that will be taking place there tomorrow. He thought it would be an appropriate venue."

"Where's the site located?" Jack asked, not recalling any mention of it in any of the reports they had obtained.

"It's directly across from the town mall."

"I hadn't realized that they had broken ground for the site," Jack said.

"We had a groundbreaking ceremony a few days

ago. Some of the building materials have already been delivered."

"What's Peter Jenkins like?" Jack asked.

Cooper gave a slight shrug. "He's an astute business man. He likes to put together deals."

"Deals?"

"He's very good at finding capital for new ventures."

"What type of ventures?" Jack questioned.

"All types. Peter specializes in finding funding for businesses. Personal or commercial, he has a knack for finding people that are willing to invest in new ideas, as long as they're financially viable. He was instrumental in finding the initial capital for the building of the new gym. He's helped quite a few small businesses in the area flourish. As a matter-of-fact, he helped Jim McCall purchase the *Aphrodite*. Jim was dead set on buying the yacht so that he could start the dinner cruises. Unfortunately, the banks in the area thought the venture too risky to take a chance on him. So, Jim went to Peter in the hope of finding the money needed for the down payment. Yachts like the *Aphrodite* don't come cheap. Finding caterers that are willing to supply food and beverages prior to payment is almost impossible. Jim needed capital and he needed it fast. Peter helped find that."

"Any idea how?"

Joe shook his head slightly. "That was never something I asked. It wasn't really any of my business."

Jack shifted slightly in his chair and picked up his now cold coffee. After draining the cup in one long swallow, he asked, "How well do you know Jim Mc-Call?"

"Fairly well. He's a great guy. He's willing to work around my school schedule so that I have a chance to study and work. He's been very support-ive."

"To you and Caryn?" Jack asked. He was trying to determine if there was any animosity on Cooper's part against McCall. If there was any way that Cooper actually believed that Caryn had an affair with the man. Jack knew that could have given Cooper a motive to murder his stepmother.

"Caryn and Jim were friends," Cooper admitted.

"Close friends?"

There was something about the way that Jack phrased the question that had Cooper looking at him curiously. "At one time, I thought so."

"What do you mean?"

Cooper took a deep breath. "There was a time when I was actually convinced that they were having an affair. I had heard stories from people about the great rapport they seemed to share whenever they were around each other. People were commenting about the easy way they communicated. I thought for sure that there had to be an underlying reason for it."

"And something changed your mind about that?" Ed asked.

There was a long pause of silence. "I found them together one night at a restaurant. I thought that Caryn was betraying my father. And make no mistake, I was furious. I even got into an argument with Caryn over it. I threatened to tell my father everything. She begged me not to. She insisted that she loved Sam and that her relationship with Jim was platonic."

"You believed her?" Jack asked.

"At the time, no. I think I mentioned to you previously that I had a problem with Caryn and my father's age difference when they first got together. I thought for sure that she had another motive for marrying him. But Jim came running to her rescue. He pretty much validated what she had said."

"And what makes you trust Jim McCall more than you trusted your stepmother?"

"The man has bailed me out on more than one occasion. When my father first started dating Caryn, I guess you could say that I gave him a hard time. In retaliation, my father stopped paying for my education. I really couldn't have afforded to miss a semester at school. I was pretty down, and one night while I was working, Jim asked me what was wrong. He gave me a loan when I explained the situation. No questions asked."

"Do you think Caryn had something to do with your father withholding your tuition?" Ed asked.

"To be honest, I'm not sure. She approached me

about it and swore that it had nothing to do with her. She offered to speak with my father in an effort to get him to loosen up a bit. Whatever she said to him must have worked. A couple of weeks later he gave me a check for tuition. I paid back Jim McCall immediately."

"And Jim McCall has had your loyalty ever since then."

"The man's been very good to me."

"Tell us, did you see Jim McCall and Caryn together recently?" Ed asked, thinking back to Tim Camp's statement about seeing them at a fast food restaurant and noticing a vehicle in the parking lot that belonged to the Coopers.

"No, I didn't. But I'm sure if they were seen together, it was innocent," Cooper said. "You never did say if you found anything else pertaining to Caryn's murder."

Ed's gaze swept over Jack and Ryan. "We don't have that many details yet. The autopsy report should be coming in some time today."

"Nothing else surfaced?"

"There was one thing," Jack replied.

"What?"

"We believe we may have found some items that we can tie to Caryn's murder."

"The anchor?" Cooper asked, having been with his father when the ankle bracelet recovered from the anchor had been identified.

"No. A heavy chain and some rope was discovered at Carrier Park. There were several strands of hair imbedded in the rope's fibers. They match Caryn's," Jack told him.

"Carrier Park," Cooper repeated, his brow wrinkled in a frown.

"Does the place mean something to you?"

"No, not to me."

"But it does to someone," Jack guessed.

Cooper's eyes met Jack's. "Tim Camp hangs out there all the time. He had asked Caryn to meet him there several times when he was trying to find out information about his father."

"How do you know that?"

"I followed Caryn a couple of times when she left the house. I was curious about who she was meeting."

"Because you didn't trust her?"

"Yes," Cooper admitted without apology. "Both times she went to the park. Tim was there waiting for her."

Ryan sat forward. "How do you know what they talked about?"

"The second time I found them there, I made it a point to accidentally run into them. Though neither one of them told me right then and there what they were talking about, Caryn told me later on that day."

"Did you believe her?" Ed questioned.

"I did. She had gotten my father to mellow

regarding my tuition payment, and her explanation about Tim just wanting information about his father made sense. If I was in the guy's shoes, I would be trying to find out information too."

"I guess anybody would," Jack agreed.

Cooper reached for his duffle bag and lifted it onto the table. "Is there anything else? I promised some friends that I would meet them down at the gym."

"We have no other questions right now," Jack said, studying the duffle bag. "I am curious though. Where did you get the duffle bag? I've been looking for one exactly like that."

Cooper looked at the bag and lifted it slightly by the handle. "This? It was a gift from Jim McCall. He gave one to all his crew last Christmas."

"Were they all the same design and color?"

"They were. He wouldn't admit it, but I assumed he got a deal on them. It comes in handy. They're very sturdy and can hold a lot of weight."

"Are they waterproof?" Ryan asked.

"Yes. Jim made sure of that. Especially since most of the crew members carry their personal belongings in them onto the yacht."

"That's a lot of bags on board the yacht. Where are they normally stored? McCall gave me a tour of the *Aphrodite* on the night we rented it for the party, but I didn't see any lockers," Ed said.

"One of the state rooms. Nobody ever has to

worry about anybody stealing anything. They were probably in the closet at the time you had the tour," Cooper said, glancing at his watch. "I don't mean to be rude but I am going to be late. If you don't have any other questions at this time, I'd better be heading out."

"Thanks for talking to us," Jack said.

"Anytime," Cooper stood up and took the bag. "Call me if you find out anything else?"

"Of course."

"I'll talk to you soon."

Jack waited until Cooper was out of earshot before he turned to Ryan and Ed. "That was enlightening."

"Yeah, it was," Ed agreed. "What did we find on Tim Camp's phone records? Any calls to Caryn Cooper?"

"Several," Jack admitted. "But the guy hasn't tried to hide the fact that he's had contact with her."

"What about the night she disappeared? Did he place any calls then?" Ed asked, taking a sip from his coffee.

"No. But he did the day before."

"So he could have arranged to meet her the night she disappeared," Ed suggested.

"He could have. The problem is that other people knew that Tim was meeting with Caryn on a regular basis," Jack replied.

"Meaning?"

"Meaning Tim makes a good scapegoat for a lot of people. Him finding the rope and chain could just be a coincidence."

"It could be."

"I'm not ruling the guy out as Caryn's killer because there are still a lot of questions surrounding him, but I think we need more answers before we focus in on one person. I don't think that we can take any chances with any of our suspects at this point," Jack said.

"So, how do you want to proceed?"

"I want to pay a call to Peter Jenkins. This is the second time his name came up and I can't help but think that the guy might be able to help us solve Caryn's murder."

"It shouldn't be hard to get an address on him." Ed called the station on his cell. "The guy's office is at the Waverly Building on Main Street."

"Are we sure it's the same Peter Jenkins?"

"Yeah. His name was on the list of friends that Joe Cooper gave you."

Jack looked at Ryan. "We'll head there first."

"And then I'd like to go to the construction site," Ryan said.

"While you two are doing that, I'll head to the station and check on the autopsy report," Ed said.

"We'll meet you back there when we're through," Jack promised.

## Chapter Twenty

The Waverly Building was a three-story modern office site comprised mostly of glass. It was relatively new to the area and all of the office space had yet to be rented, so human traffic entering and leaving the building was relatively light.

Jack parked in front, in one of the spaces reserved for visitors, and cast a quick glance at his watch. "It's early yet. There's a chance that Jenkins won't be here." He stepped out of the car.

Ryan quickly joined him. "There's also a chance that he's a workaholic and gets here at sunrise."

A cold blast of air conditioning hit them as soon they entered the lobby, and they made their way over to the receptionist's desk.

Jack took out his badge and asked to talk to Peter Jenkins.

A well-groomed, middle-aged woman in stylish suit looked at the detectives curiously. After phoning his office, she said, "He'll be with you shortly. If you'll have a seat."

They took up the offer and Jack said, "I'm surprised that there's not more people mulling around here."

"If I remember correctly, the building was only completed a couple of months ago. Judging by appearances, I doubt the rent around here is cheap," Ryan said, his gaze straying to the elevator.

Upon hearing the bell that signaled the elevator door was opening, Jack was surprised to find Sam Cooper exiting the lift beside a distinguished looking, gray-haired man in a three-piece suit. Jack immediately knew the identity of the man beside Cooper. It had to be Jenkins.

Rising to his feet, he waited for the men to approach.

Cooper was surprised to greet the detectives at Peter Jenkins' office.

Jack acknowledged Cooper before greeting the man beside him. "You must be Peter Jenkins."

Jenkins immediately took Jack's hand in a firm handshake. "I am."

"We were wondering if we could have a moment of your time," Jack said. "Unless right now isn't convenient."

"No, it's fine," Jenkins said. "Sam was just leaving."

"I am," Cooper said. "I only came by because we're holding a memorial service for Caryn tomorrow. I brought Peter the photograph that will be used during the ceremony."

"We ran into your son this morning at a restaurant. He explained about the service," Jack told him.

Cooper nodded. "I know. He called to tell me that he had run into you. He also told me about the additional evidence that surfaced last night."

"We were going to contact you later this morning to talk to you about that." Cooper's pale and haggard appearance gave Jack the impression that he had slept little since his wife disappeared. But Jack also sensed that Jenkins was watching the exchange between them closely, and he didn't want to risk saying anything in front of the man that might compromise the investigation. "We would like to talk to you, but perhaps now wouldn't be the best time. Can you come to the police station around noon?"

Cooper bit back a protest at the delay, understanding that Jack wanted to have the discussion in private. "I'll be there."

"Good. We can discuss everything then."

Cooper turned to Peter Jenkins. "I'll see you tomorrow morning."

"Call me if you need anything."

Jenkins waited until Cooper left the building

before turning to Jack and Ryan. "Why don't we go up to my office. We'll have a little more privacy there," he said, leading the way.

Five minutes later, Jack and Ryan were seated in Jenkins' office. The man had stepped away for a brief moment to have a word with his administrative assistant and after he returned he closed the door to the office and took a seat. "Sorry about that. I wanted to make sure that my assistant knew that I didn't want to be disturbed. So tell me, what can I do for you?" he asked, leaning back in his leather chair.

"We understand you know Jim McCall as well as the Coopers," Jack replied without hesitation.

"I do."

"Do you mind if I ask how close you are to the Coopers?"

"I consider Sam a very good friend."

"And did you consider Caryn a friend also?"

"I did."

"Can you tell us when you spoke to Caryn last?"

"About a week ago. I ran into her at a luncheon for the new gym."

"Was her husband there also?" Ryan asked.

Jenkins shook his head. "No, Sam couldn't make it that day. He had another business meeting to attend."

"So Caryn was there alone?"

"I believe she came alone, but there were plenty of

people there for her to talk to. She didn't lack company."

"Who did she talk to?" Jack questioned.

"Several people actually. Jim McCall and Joe Cooper to name a few. Both were seated at her table. Why? Is it important?"

"It might be. We're trying to determine if there was anybody present that might have had a problem with Caryn Cooper. Anybody there who might have wished her harm."

Jenkins was shaking his head before Jack finished speaking. "I can tell you right now that everybody at that luncheon held Caryn in the highest regard. She was well liked by everyone who knew her."

"You sound sure of that."

"I am."

"Are you aware of how Caryn's body was discovered?"

"Yes. I was as shocked as anyone when I learned that her body was brought on board Jim McCall's boat."

"How well do you know McCall?" Ryan asked.

"How well?" Jenkins frowned as he pondered the question. "I consider him a friend. I've known him since grade school. His family lived down the street from mine."

"In your estimation, how well did he know Caryn?"

"I know they were friendly whenever I saw them

together." Jenkins looked at Ryan curiously. "I'm not sure just how well they knew each other."

"Did you notice anything that would suggest they were more than casual acquaintances?" Jack asked.

"No, I didn't. Why are you asking so many questions about Jim McCall?"

Jack didn't want to say anything to Jenkins that might make its way back to McCall. "We're just covering bases. Jim McCall was on deck when the body was discovered. He showed no sign of recognition once Caryn was brought on board the boat."

Jenkins was quiet for a moment before stating, "I would imagine that he was in shock that a body was discovered."

"Possibly," Jack allowed.

"Jim McCall is a very honorable man. I'm quite sure that if he would have recognized Caryn he would have mentioned it. Maybe with everything going on in his life right now, he was a little distracted."

"Meaning he had other things on his mind that night?" Ryan prompted.

"I would say so."

"Do you have any idea of what that could have been?" Jack asked.

There was a long pause. "I might. I helped secure the financing for the *Aphrodite*. There was a balloon payment coming due. Jim was having difficulty coming up with the money."

Jack couldn't help but pay attention to the words. "How do you know that?"

"I spoke with Jim several days ago. He was distraught to say the least. He asked if I could help him obtain an extension on the loan. According to what he told me, he had a few cruises going out this week and he should have been able to have the full amount of money within seven days."

"So?" Ryan prompted.

"So, he came up with the money a lot sooner than he expected, and I had nothing to do with it."

"How much sooner?"

"It was only a couple of days after I originally spoke to him about the extension."

"Which would have been . . ." Jack prompted.

"The day before Caryn disappeared."

"Did he mention anything to you about how he came by the money?"

"No. But to be honest, I didn't ask. The investment wasn't mine to keep track of. I didn't think it was appropriate to ask him how he obtained the money."

Jack leaned back in his chair and studied Jenkins. There was a hesitation in the man's voice that indicated he was withholding some information. "But you have an idea of how he came up with the money," he guessed.

"I have some thoughts."

"Anything you'd care to share?"

"I don't have anything to substantiate them."

"We'd appreciate any information you can offer, validated or not."

Jenkins was quiet while he considered Jack's request.

"Mr. Jenkins . . ."

"I'll tell you what I can," he finally said.

Jack sensed that the man's reluctance to speak was more out of a misguided sense of loyalty than anything else. "Whatever you say will remain confidential."

Jenkins studied Jack quietly for a moment, almost as if he was trying to judge his sincerity. "I think he may have gotten the money from Sam Cooper."

"Why do you say that?"

"Just a hunch. I have a friend down at the bank who took care of the paperwork on Jim's original loan. He was the one who called me to tell me that the loan had been paid in full."

"And?"

"And he made the comment that the funds used to pay the loan were transferred from a personal account at the bank."

"Did your friend actually say it was Sam Cooper who transferred the money?"

"No. He wouldn't. That would have been a break in trust."

Jack shook his head slightly. "Then I don't understand. What makes you think that Sam Cooper paid off the loan?"

"Because I was in the bank on the morning that Jim's loan was paid off. I saw Jim there talking to Sam."

"Did either of the men see you at the bank?"

"I don't think so."

"Did you approach them?"

"No. Their conversation looked a little intense."

"Intense?"

"A little heated," Jenkins explained. "I can't be sure, but it looked like they may have been arguing over something."

Jack sat back in his chair. "Let me ask you something. Was Caryn Cooper at the bank that day also?"

"Not inside. But when I was leaving, I saw her waiting by the car in the parking lot."

"Was she alone?"

"No. She was talking to Tim Camp."

## Chapter Twenty-one

Thirty minutes later, Jack and Ryan walked out of the Waverly Building, contemplating the new information.

"So what do you think?" Ryan asked.

"I'm not sure. I don't like the fact that Jenkins claims to have seen Sam Cooper and Jim McCall talking together at the bank."

"Because of Sam Cooper's jealousy?"

"Jealous rage may be a possibility of how Caryn Cooper was killed. Maybe Sam confronted Jim about his relationship with Caryn. We won't know for sure until we see the actual autopsy report, but the possibility does exist that Sam could have been responsible for his wife's death," Jack said.

"He seemed willing to cooperate when we went to his house to speak with him after her body was identified."

Jack shot him a look. "Wouldn't you if you were trying to cover up a heinous crime?"

Ryan grunted. "Well, at least we have one thing in our favor at the moment."

"What?"

"The guy promised he would come down to the police station at noon. We have enough time to check out the construction site to see if there's anything there before we have to head back to the station to meet him."

"And the sooner we do that, the better off we'll be. Especially if Sam and Joe Cooper visited the site yesterday."

Fifteen minutes later, Jack parked across the street from the construction site that had already broken ground. Cement and steel beams as well as wooden planks were carefully laid out on the property that had been surveyed and roped off, and a high metal chainlink fence surrounded the area.

Stepping out of the car, Jack took a moment to examine the site. "They have a lot of the building materials in place."

Ryan walked around the car to Jack. "It seems like a strange place to hold a memorial service."

Jack silently agreed. The area looked like an active construction site. Heavy equipment was standing stationary, and with the other building materials stacked, Jack couldn't envision any type of service there.

Walking around the fenced area, Jack stopped when he found a place where they could enter. "Over here, Ryan. Somebody already cut the links to get into the area."

"Probably kids."

Jack agreed, stepping onto the ground that was leveled with poured concrete. He walked around the perimeter of the foundation, pausing when something caught his attention. "Come look at this."

Ryan walked over. Looking down at the spot Jack indicated, he noticed several signatures in the cement. He crouched down. "It looks like the committee wanted to leave their mark."

Jack studied the three-foot-square area that held the signatures of the committee members.

"Both Caryn and Sam Cooper were here," Ryan stated. "That probably means that Joe was here also. But the question is, who else was?" He walked over to where the wooden planks were roped together. He examined the rope's thickness. "I can't be a hundred percent sure, but it looks like the rope used to secure this lumber is similar in size to the rope Tim Camp found at Carrier Park."

Jack frowned and had a look. "We'll have the lab take a look at it," he said, reaching into his suit jacket for a pocket knife and cutting off a sample.

Ryan continued to search the area. "There's a lot of heavy plastic around here," he said, noticing the sheets that were used as a barrier between the ground and the building materials. "It looks identical to the plastic sheets that were in one of the boxes that we took from Jim McCall's residence."

"Maybe the guy took them from this site. We already know that he attended a fundraising luncheon for the new gym. It's possible he was here for the groundbreaking ceremony."

"It would make sense. Especially since from outward appearances he also seemed to have an interest in Caryn Cooper."

"From the looks of the home renovation project going on at his house, he was going to need a lot of materials. If he was here and mentioned the work he was doing, it's possible someone offered him some supplies," Jack said, doing a final walk-through of the construction site. "Do you see anything else here that we should be looking at before we head back to the station?"

"No, I'm ready to go. I'm curious if the lab will be able to match the sample of rope you took to the one that was found at Carrier Park."

"Let's start back so that we can have the lab technicians take a look at it." Jack was just about to step through the opening of the fence when a piece of metal caught his eye. "Ryan, come over here."

Ryan watched as Jack bent down to retrieve something out of the dirt. "What did you find?"

"This," Jack said, showing a brass zipper pull.

Ryan looked at the object. "I'm sure there have been a lot of people on this site. There's no telling when that was left."

"Do you have an evidence bag on you?"

"Of course," Ryan said, removing a small plastic bag from his suit jacket and handing it to Jack. "Do you really think this has anything to do with this case?"

"I'm not sure, but I think that's the same type of pull that was on Joe Cooper's duffle bag this morning."

"So?"

"The bag found on the *Aphrodite* was missing a zipper pull."

## Chapter Twenty-two

Ed was at his desk doing paperwork when Jack and Ryan walked into the detectives' room. Looking up, he caught their eye and waved them into his office. "I'm glad you two are finally here. Take a seat."

"Why? What did you come up with?" Jack asked.

Ed picked up a manila folder. "They finished the autopsy on Caryn Cooper. The medical examiner discovered a contusion on the back of her head that wasn't readily noticeable because it was covered by her hair."

"Was the injury what caused her death?" Jack asked, reaching for the report.

"No. The cause of death was asphyxiation."

"By drowning?" Ryan asked.

"No, not drowning. There wasn't water in her lungs. She was dead before she was put in the water."

"She could have been suffocated in her sleep," Jack suggested.

Ryan leaned back in his chair. "That would mean that either Sam or Joe Cooper were responsible. There are other suspects. We can't lose sight of the fact that there was a lot of plastic at the construction site. She could have been killed there and her body transported and dumped in the Long Island Sound."

Ed frowned. "The site where the gym was being built?"

"Yeah. We stopped by to take a look at the place. The building materials and construction equipment are already on-site," Ryan told him.

"That's an odd place to have a memorial service then."

"That's what we thought. But that's definitely what's supposed to take place tomorrow. We confirmed it with Peter Jenkins and Sam Cooper," Jack said as he finished reading the report and handed it to Ryan.

"When did you see Sam Cooper?" Ed asked.

"At Jenkins' office. He said he was there to discuss the arrangements for the memorial service."

"Kind of early for Cooper to be there," Ed murmured.

Jack shrugged. "From what we've been given to

understand, the man's always been an early riser. But we did find out something that we need to look into. According to Jenkins, there's a chance that Cooper and McCall might have conducted some type of business together."

"What type of business?"

"Apparently McCall was having some financial problems, and a balloon note on his loan for the *Aphrodite* was coming due. Jenkins believes that Cooper might have offered assistance with making the payment," Jack told him.

Ed reached for a pen and tapped it on his desk top. "Why would he do that?"

"Well, that's the million dollar question. And one that we should find out the answer to within the next two hours."

"What do you mean?"

"Cooper promised to come in at noon to talk to us. He's interested in what we found out about his wife's murder. Based on what we just learned from the autopsy report, I think it will be interesting to see his reaction to the fact that his wife didn't drown. We should be able to at least determine if he had anything to do with her death."

It was five minutes to twelve when Jack's intercom buzzed. He told Ryan, "Sam Cooper's here. They're showing him into the conference room now. Do you want to head over to meet him? I'll let Ed know he's here and then I'll join you."

"Sure. I'll see you there in a few minutes."

Cooper was already seated at the conference table when Jack and Ed arrived, a cup of coffee laid out before him.

"You remember Captain Stall, don't you?" Jack asked, knowing that Ed had met with the man when Cooper had identified the ankle bracelet embedded in the anchor.

"Of course," Cooper said. "Joe told me about your conversation this morning. About the evidence that was found at Carrier Park."

"We also received the official results from Caryn's autopsy report today," Jack said.

"And?" Cooper's hand tightened noticeably on his cup of coffee, the knuckles turning white.

"The official cause of death is asphyxiation."

Cooper frowned. "From drowning?"

"No. From all indications, Caryn was suffocated."

Cooper shook his head in confusion. "But I don't understand. How?"

"That we're not sure of as of yet. At the moment, two possibilities of how your wife was murdered come to mind. The first being that her air flow was cut off with a sheet of plastic or a bag of some sort."

"And the other possibility?"

"The other possibility would be that your wife was

murdered in her sleep. Suffocated. Possibly by a pillow being held over her face," Jack said.

Cooper sat weakly back in his chair and released his hold on his coffee cup. "I didn't kill Caryn," he murmured faintly.

"Nobody said you did." Jack couldn't afford to alienate Cooper, they needed his cooperation. They had no proof that the woman had been suffocated in her sleep. It was just a theory. Jack wasn't willing to make any accusations until they had some sort of proof.

"I loved Caryn. I would never do anything to hurt her," Cooper insisted, his hands clenched together on the table.

"We're not disputing that. But we need your help to solve Caryn's murder. Tell us who would want to see her dead."

"I don't know."

"Think, Mr. Cooper, who had a motive to kill your wife?"

"I don't know! As far as I know, everybody liked Caryn."

"Including your son?" Ryan asked.

Cooper's eyes shot immediately to Ryan's. "Joe wouldn't have harmed Caryn. He would never do anything to hurt me."

"But how did he relate to Caryn directly? How well did they get along?"

Cooper ran a hand through his hair and rising from

his chair, he moved over to the window to look outside. "They weren't friends, but I wouldn't classify them as enemies. Joe had no reason to want Caryn dead. She wasn't a threat to him. His future was secure. He's well educated and has a trust fund to see him through any hard times."

"Joe received a call on his cell phone on the night Caryn disappeared. It originated from your house. Did you call your son?" Jack asked.

Cooper shook his head. "Caryn did. She had gone down to the kitchen for a drink and she realized that we were running low on milk. She called Joe to ask if he would pick up a gallon from the convenience store on the way home. The one in our neighborhood is open twenty-four hours."

"Did he bring home the milk?"

"It was there the next morning."

"But did you actually see Joe when he came home?"

"No. But he wouldn't hurt Caryn," Cooper said, taking offense at Jack's words. "He had no motive to want to kill her."

"Somebody had a motive, Mr. Cooper. Help us figure out who did."

"If I had any idea of who was responsible for Caryn's murder, I would tell you," Cooper said, getting more agitated by the moment.

There was a noticeable strain on his facial features and his hands kept clenching and unclenching into fists, almost as if he needed some sort of outlet for his emotions.

"Mr. Cooper, are you all right?"

"What?"

"Are you all right? Would you like us to call someone for you? Would you be more comfortable with your attorney present?"

Cooper was shaking his head before Jack finished the last question. "No. I have nothing to hide. I want to help in this investigation. I just don't know how."

Ed expelled a short breath and motioned to the chair that Cooper had vacated. "Why don't you sit down and we'll work through this together. We have a list of people that we need some information on. People that we have questions about. We'll take each name on an individual basis and you can tell us if there's anything in the person's past with Caryn that we should look into."

Cooper nodded and returned to his seat.

"Let's start with Kate Walter," Jack said. "I understand that Caryn had once accused her of theft."

"That's not true. That's not what happened."

"Then tell us what did happen."

Cooper ran a shaky hand down his face and reached for his cup of coffee. He took a long sip before he responded. "Kate is a friend of Joe's. Caryn didn't like her. She thought maybe she was just hanging around to use him."

"Use him? In what way?" Ryan asked.

"Financially. Caryn always suspected Kate's motives. She didn't understand how Kate and Joe could be just friends. She thought for sure that Kate was using Joe to achieve a lifestyle that she wanted."

"Meaning?"

"Fancy dinners. Nights on the town."

"What was your take on it?" Ed asked.

"I think they were just friends. Kate and Joe have known each other a long time. They understood each other. They were comfortable with each other. To be honest, I wouldn't be surprised if they ended up together one day."

Jack's eyes narrowed. "Was jewelry actually missing when Caryn made the accusation?"

"No. I had taken Caryn's pearl necklace to have the pearls restrung. It was supposed to have been a surprise for her. I had no idea that she would accuse Kate of taking the necklace, and I was shocked when I found out. She apologized to Kate that very evening."

"Did Kate accept the apology?" Ryan asked.

"She said she did. I believed her. She was over the house with Joe several times after that, and she never gave any indication that she was still bothered by what Caryn had said."

"Fair enough," Jack said. "What about Tim Camp?"

"Tim? What about him?"

"Caryn had been married to his father. Could he have resented her so much that he would want to harm her?"

Cooper was quiet for a long moment. "I don't know. I don't think so. He never gave any indication that he would."

"He was speaking to her the other day at the bank, wasn't he?" Jack asked, recalling that Jenkins claimed to have seen them together.

Cooper looked surprised that Jack would know that. "Yes, he was. I had gone to the bank to take care of some business, and Tim left the building as I was going in. I saw him go over to the car to talk to Caryn."

"Do you have any idea of what they were talking about?"

"Not really. Just what Caryn told me."

"Which was?" Ed pressed.

"Just that he came over to say hello, and that he was looking forward to the groundbreaking cere-mony for the gym that afternoon."

"He was there?" Jack asked.

"Yes. A lot of people were."

"Did Tim have any ties to the project?"

"Not really. I think he went more out of respect for Caryn."

Jack recalled something that McCall had men-tioned to them when they searched his house. About how Cooper didn't like Caryn socializing with other people. "Did you ever ask Caryn not to talk to Tim?" he asked, wanting to know if there was any truth to it.

"No. I admit that I wanted Caryn's full attention,

and that it bothered me at first that Tim was contacting her so much. But I understood Tim's needs for answers."

"You said it bothered you at first," Jack said. "What made you change your mind?"

"My son Joe. He explained to me that if he had been in Tim's shoes that he probably would have been doing the same thing. It made sense."

Jack nodded. "You said that Tim was at the groundbreaking ceremony. Was Jim McCall also there?"

"He was. I didn't get a chance to talk to him, but I did see him speaking to Caryn, as well as Tim. He was probably there in support of Tim and Joe."

Jack studied Cooper. For a man that admitted to feeling jealous about Caryn, he gave no indication that he considered McCall a threat. Which meant that if there had been something going on between McCall and Caryn, Cooper might not have been aware of it. Hoping Cooper would reveal more details, Jack said, "McCall seems to have a solid relationship with his employees."

"Especially Tim."

"Why do you say that?"

"I think Tim thought of him as a father figure."

Ryan frowned. "I don't understand. He had a father."

"Yes, but it was one who never paid any attention to him," Cooper reminded him.

"What was the connection that Tim Camp and McCall shared?" Jack asked.

"Jim McCall was good friends with Tim's mother, Carol. They had even dated a while after Roger Camp left her."

"Was the relationship serious?"

"At one time. It didn't last though. I think they figured out that they made better friends."

"Was Caryn aware of the relationship between Jim McCall and Tim's mother?" Jack asked.

"Yes. I think she secretly wished that it would work out between the two of them."

"Why do you say that?"

"Because she wanted them both to be happy."

The ease that Cooper displayed while making the simple statement led credibility to it. Jack considered all that the man had revealed. He had shed a lot of light on the other suspects. But there was one question that hadn't been answered yet. "Why did you pay off McCall's loan on the *Aphrodite*?"

The man was startled. "How do you know about that?"

"Then it's true?"

"Yes," Cooper admitted slowly.

"Who asked you to pay off the loan? McCall or Caryn?"

"McCall did. He offered me a percentage of ownership in the *Aphrodite* if I did. When I approached

Caryn about it and discussed it with her, she thought it would be a good investment."

"She had an interest in the yacht?" Ed questioned.

"We rented it one night for a party. She enjoyed it. I think she fell in love with the idea of possibly owning something along that nature. She was full of ideas that night about how to improve it. Of how lucrative it could be if it was run right. She thought it would be a good investment for Joe's future."

"Do you know if she mentioned any of that to Mc-Call?" Jack asked. He didn't get the impression that McCall would have willingly let anyone take over the running of the *Aphrodite*.

"I'm not sure. Why? Would it matter?"

"I don't know. That's a question that still remains to be answered." Jack said.

"Caryn and Jim respected one another. As a matter of fact, we all had lunch together the other day. Caryn and I stopped in a fast food restaurant for a quick bite, and Jim was there. He kept Caryn company while I answered a business call on my cell phone."

"Do you know what they discussed?"

"I can't be a hundred percent sure, but I think it was the progress of the new gym. Jim seemed very interested in the project."

Jack waited a moment to see if Cooper would offer anything further. When he wasn't going to, Jack said, "We appreciate you being so forthcoming. And I want to assure you that we will find the person responsible for your wife's murder."

Cooper relaxed slightly. "Did you have any other questions right now?"

"Do you have anything else that you believe may be helpful?"

"No, but I'll call you if I can think of anything."

"We'd appreciate that."

"And you'll do likewise?"

"Of course."

"Then, I should be heading out. I promised Joe I would meet him for a late lunch."

"Well, what do you think?" Ed asked the moment Cooper left.

"I think Ryan and I will be going to the memorial service tomorrow. All of our possible suspects should be in attendance. With any luck, whoever murdered Caryn Cooper will do something that will pinpoint them as the person responsible for her murder," Jack replied, rising from his own chair. "But for now, I'm going to head over to the lab and see if they had a chance to analyze the piece of rope and the zipper pull that we picked up at the construction site this afternoon."

## Chapter Twenty-three

The following morning, Jack and Ryan were at Caryn Cooper's memorial service, watching as the guests arrived. The fence that had protected the area the day before had been removed for the occasion, and white folding wooden chairs were strategically placed around what was to be the main entrance to the gym. Floral arrangements were positioned around Caryn's commemorative photo, and a podium stood off to the side. At the moment, soft chamber music was being piped into the area, while a technician performed a last-minute sound check with the microphone.

Standing off to the side, Jack observed the activity and thought about the evidence that was uncovered yesterday. The zipper pull he found at the construction site turned out to be a match to the duffle bag on Jim McCall's yacht, which Jack expected. But something more important showed. The sample of rope from the construction site matched the one found at Carrier Park. Jack thought there was a good chance that the duffle bag had held the rope that was used by Caryn Cooper's murderer. It would at least explain why the bag had been hidden in the engine compartment. It had to contain something that the owner didn't want found.

Based on a review of the evidence, Jack, Ryan, and Ed determined that Caryn's murderer must have been present on McCall's yacht on the night her body was found. Which narrowed down the suspects to three: McCall, Tim Camp, and Kate Walter. One of those three people had to have been responsible for Caryn's death, and Jack was betting it was one of the men. The person who killed Caryn had to be strong enough to carry her body on board the boat. They had to know enough about the ship's layout to keep the body hidden until an opportunity presented itself to dispose of it in Long Island Sound. And they had to have the ability to keep any emotional turmoil under control. Kate wasn't strong enough to carry the body on her own, her build was too slight. And she was easy to read. But McCall and Camp were more than capable of carrying out the task. And both men had suspicion focused on them due to their relationship with Caryn.

As mourners filed past, Jack and Ryan paid attention to the interaction between Sam Cooper and the people that came to pay their respects. The amount of mourners was impressive, and it was an indication of just how respected Caryn and Sam Cooper were within the community.

"Sam Cooper seems to be on friendly terms with everyone in attendance so far," Ryan murmured.

"Yeah, he does." Jack glanced off to the side at Joe Cooper and noticed he sat quietly, his eyes focused on Caryn's photograph by the podium. "Too bad the same can't be said for his offspring."

"He does look a little quiet."

"And he's not the only one." Jack looked at Camp, who had arrived unobtrusively. "Tim barely acknowledged Sam Cooper just now."

Ryan studied Camp. The paleness of Camp's features stood out in stark contrast against the dark navy color of his suit, and sunglasses shielded his eyes, though the morning was gray and overcast. "He definitely looks like he's in mourning."

"Or shock. I'm not sure which." Jack watched as Camp paused by Caryn's photograph and stood there for several minutes before he took his seat. He wondered what the man was thinking about.

Jack was so intent on watching Camp that he almost missed McCall's arrival. The man walked through the entrance and took a seat immediately. He didn't stop to talk to Sam Cooper, nor did he approach Joe

Cooper or Camp. Instead, he sat down in the last row of chairs. McCall's lack of interaction with other people had Jack looking at him curiously. Suspiciously.

He considered what he knew of McCall, or rather what he was led to believe. The man supposedly had a friendly relationship with Joe Cooper and Camp. He also was given money by Sam Cooper to pay off the loan against the *Aphrodite*. It didn't make sense that he was keeping himself isolated. It didn't make sense that he didn't acknowledge anybody in the Cooper family.

As Jack stood there watching the man, Walter arrived. Unlike McCall, Camp, and the youngest Cooper, there was nothing discreet about her arrival. She stopped by Sam Cooper and embraced him in a comforting hug before she moved over to Joe Cooper and took a seat beside him, her hand reaching out to clasp his in what Jack assumed was a gesture of comfort. She glanced over at Camp and smiled before she turned to lift a hand in greeting to McCall. But McCall didn't acknowledge her.

"Jim McCall's lost in his own world," Jack spoke softly to Ryan so that he wouldn't be overheard.

"Yeah, I noticed that. Either he's so consumed with grief that he can't concentrate, or he has something else on his mind."

"Possibly the way Caryn Cooper died," Jack suggested, just as Sam Cooper began to walk up to the podium.

The crowd fell silent, and the lingering guests quickly took their seats in preparation for the service.

Cooper waited until everybody was seated. Gripping the sides of the wooden podium, he cleared his throat. "I'd like to thank you for attending today."

Jack observed how Joe Cooper and Kate sat together, gripping each other's hands, while their attention focused on Sam Cooper's words. Though Joe wasn't overly expressive in his facial expressions, Jack had no doubt that the man was there in full support of his father. And Kate seemed to be there in support of Joe.

Camp sat alone, an empty chair beside him, but he was also paying careful attention to Cooper's words. He gave no outward indication that he was preoccupied by any other thoughts. As Jack's gaze swept around the other guests in attendance, he realized that there was only one person who seemed distracted. And that was McCall.

As Jack watched McCall, he noticed that the man's attention was focused on the building supplies and construction equipment that had been moved out of the way for the service. Jack glanced over at the area that held the man's interest, trying to determine exactly what it was that he was looking at. He noticed the steel beams that had been at the site yesterday, as well as the heavy dark tarp that covered them in an effort to clean up the area for the memorial service. The tarp caught Jack's attention. There was something familiar about it.

His mind flashed back to the night on the yacht when Caryn's body had been discovered. He thought about the way the police officers at the party had been able to keep everyone off the deck with the exception of one person. McCall.

At the time, Jack really didn't think too much about the man's insistence that he be present. It was his yacht after all. It made sense that he would want to help. But as Jack thought about everything that had transpired that night, he had a sudden image of the tarp that McCall had brought on deck for Caryn's body to be laid on. It matched the tarp that covered the steel beams, and the type that McCall used in his home renovation project.

The identical pieces of rope found at the beach and at the man's house and the matching tarps suggested McCall might have helped himself to items from the construction site. And if that was the case, it stood to reason that the man would have needed something to transport the items. In all likelihood, he wouldn't have wanted to take any chances that his actions would be noticed. He wouldn't have wanted to be accused of theft.

Jack thought about the duffle bag discovered in the engine compartment on McCall's yacht, a bag that according to Joe Cooper, McCall had purchased in bulk. It made sense that McCall would have kept one for himself, just as it made sense that he would have known of an out of the way place to hide the bag so that another one of his employees wouldn't accidentally pick it up, thinking that it was their own.

As Jack reviewed everything, he couldn't help but think that McCall had something to do with Caryn's death. Though the evidence that pointed to him was strictly circumstantial, there were too many coincidences, too many unanswered questions that revolved around the man.

Jack suspected McCall didn't claim knowing Caryn on the night her body was discovered because he didn't want to draw undue attention to himself. He had to have known that if he had acknowledged knowing her that he would have immediately come under scrutiny that very night. Which was something he wasn't prepared for. He wanted the chance to clean up any evidence that could possibly tie him to Caryn's death.

A pause of silence had Jack's attention refocusing briefly on the podium. Sam Cooper had finished speaking and resumed his seat, and Joe Cooper stood and walked over to the microphone. But at the same time Joe arrived at the podium, McCall rose from his own chair and left the memorial service.

Jack nudged Ryan. "Let's follow him," Jack murmured softly.

## Chapter Twenty-four

Jack and Ryan followed McCall to his yacht, *Aphrodite,* being careful to keep a respectable distance behind the man so he wouldn't realize he was being tailed.

They noticed he didn't hesitate when he exited his vehicle. His attention seemed distracted. He barely seemed to notice a large group of teenagers gathered by the water's edge that he almost walked into. In fact, he didn't even glance in their direction. He appeared totally lost in his own thoughts as he stepped onto the wooden dock and quickly made his way over to his yacht, leaped on, and disappeared from view.

"Let's go," Jack said.

As Jack and Ryan neared the *Aphrodite*, they

listened for the sound of any voices, curious if McCall was meeting anyone or if he was alone. But the empty deck and the quietness was an indication there was no one else on board. Quickly, before McCall noticed them, Jack and Ryan stepped onto the yacht. Just then the engines sprang to life and McCall came down the side of the vessel, preparing to take off. He stopped short when he came to the detectives.

"What are you doing here?" McCall asked sharply, quickly masking his shock.

"We were at Caryn Cooper's memorial service and we saw you there. When you left rather abruptly, we were concerned that something might be wrong," Jack improvised.

McCall didn't respond, but the way his body tensed was proof he was disconcerted to have been under close scrutiny.

"Mr. McCall," Ryan said, "are you all right?"

McCall expelled a harsh breath. "I'm fine. And this really isn't a good time. So if you'll excuse me . . ." He gestured with his right hand that they should vacate the yacht.

Jack and Ryan made no move.

"We have a few questions for you. I promise we'll only take a few minutes of your time." Jack didn't know what he would do if the man refused. They had no warrant for McCall's arrest. Jack was just following his gut instincts.

After a long moment, McCall sighed and ran a

weary hand across the back of his neck. "Look, this has been a rough day for me. As a matter of fact, it's been a rough couple of days. If it's all the same to you, your questions will have to wait until a later time."

"I'm afraid this can't wait," Jack said.

"What do you mean?"

"The questions that we need answered pertain to Caryn Cooper's murder."

"I already told you everything I know. If you want me to repeat it, I'll be happy to come down to the po-lice station later this afternoon. But right now, I just need to get away for a while."

"So we gathered."

"Then if you don't mind . . ." McCall gestured once more to the dock.

"What we'd like to ask you won't take long," Jack said. He casually began walking toward the front of the yacht, forcing McCall to talk to them.

McCall quickly followed. "Detective Reeves . . ."

"Is this where you did it?" Jack asked, stopping at the point on the yacht where he believed Caryn Cooper's body might have been thrown overboard. It was an isolated place, an area that wouldn't have been under scrutiny. It was far enough away from the main dining salon and the surrounding deck, so that any action wouldn't have been observed.

McCall shook his head in confusion. "Did what?"

"Dump Caryn Cooper's body over the side of the *Aphrodite*," Jack replied calmly. He wanted to get a rise out of McCall, and the only way he felt that he would be able to do that was to make a direct attack. McCall was too controlled to slip and say something incriminating without some sort of jolt. Jack knew from experience that sometimes the only way to get the truth from someone was to blindside them.

McCall went completely still for a moment before he gained control. Reaching up, he removed his sunglasses. "I'm not quite sure what you're implying, detective."

"Don't you?" Jack walked over to one of the rails and looked over the side into the vast expanse of Long Island Sound. "How easy was it to dump Caryn's body overboard while you had a boatload of people?"

When McCall didn't reply, Jack continued the verbal assault. "How did you get Caryn Cooper on board without anybody seeing her? Did you keep her body wrapped in the tarp that you so conveniently found on the night we discovered the body? Is that why the material was so handy?"

"You don't know what you're talking about," McCall ground out, his knuckles turning white as he gripped his hands into fists.

Jack couldn't help but notice McCall wasn't forcing the issue of getting them to leave the boat. It was a strong indication that he had managed to hit a nerve. He decided to push his advantage. "Don't we?"

"No! I would never do anything to hurt Caryn. I had no reason to."

"You would if she was threatening to take away control of the *Aphrodite*."

"But she wasn't."

"No, her husband, Sam, was."

McCall shook his head. "You're wrong."

"We have evidence to the contrary."

"Sam Cooper had no right to anything having to do with the *Aphrodite*," McCall ground out, losing some of the control he was trying so hard to hold on to.

"Even after he paid off your balloon payment on the loan?" Jack questioned.

"How do you know about that?"

"Does it matter? It's true, isn't it?"

"It is. But it's immaterial. Sam Cooper had no rights to the *Aphrodite*. I never made any agreement with regards to my business."

"But that's not how the Coopers understood things, was it? And that's what prompted Caryn's murder. You found out about Sam's plan to take over the running of the *Aphrodite*."

Stunned silence followed Jack's statement.

Jack saw the muscle that was ticking involuntarily in McCall's jaw, the stiffening of his posture. Jack knew in that moment that McCall was aware of the Coopers' plan to take over the *Aphrodite*. There was no instant denial, no alternative explanation.

"You didn't realize that Sam was doing it on Caryn's request, did you?" Jack continued to assail. "So you asked Caryn to come and talk to you. You were hoping that you could convince her to keep Sam from following through on his plan. And that's when you found out that it was actually Caryn's idea to take over your business, not her husband's. That she had her own objectives." Jack paused for a moment to let his words sink in. "What happened when you found that out? Did things get rough?"

McCall's jaw clenched, causing his tan to whiten. But when he spoke, his voice was controlled. "You don't know what you're talking about."

"I think I do."

"You have no proof that anything you're claiming happened," McCall stated harshly, turning and walking across the deck. He looked out over the water briefly before he turned and leaned back against the railing, his arms crossed as he faced the detectives.

Jack studied McCall. The man was right. They had no real proof. At least not yet. But a confession from the man would be enough to close this case, and Jack sensed that if he pushed hard enough, if he enraged the man enough, he might be able to get that. "Don't we?" he taunted.

There was a pause before McCall spoke. "I think you're just spinning your wheels, detective. Instead of staying here and insulting me, why don't you go out and find Caryn's real killer?"

"Why don't you cooperate with us?"

"I've done nothing but cooperate. Exactly what is it that you want from me?"

"For starters, why don't you tell us the truth about where you were on the night of Caryn's disappearance."

"I was home."

"The truth," Jack demanded.

"I . . . was . . . home," McCall repeated.

Jack expelled a silent sigh. He would have to find a different way to get answers. A different way to get the confession that he knew McCall could give. "Was that before or after you suffocated Caryn?"

McCall leaned weakly back against the railing. "Suffocated?"

"Did you think she died from the blow to the head?" Jack asked, noticing the despair on McCall's face, the look of shock he couldn't hide. He sensed by McCall's reaction a moment ago that Caryn's death might have been an accident. McCall was too shaken by the realization that she died by suffocation. He was hoping that McCall was off balance enough so that he could get the answers they needed. Knowing that he would have to push McCall further, Jack walked over to the engine compartment where the search team had found the duffle bag. Crouching down, he lifted the cover. "Did you keep Caryn's body in here, along with the anchor used to weigh down her body? Things didn't go according to plan that night, did they? You didn't expect the anchor to separate from her body. You thought that the chain and rope you used were enough to secure her limbs. You didn't realize that the hook on the chain wasn't secure. That it would separate from the anchor. That in your haste to dispose of the body, you failed to secure the knot on the rope that bound her wrists to the chain."

Not giving McCall a chance to respond, Jack rose to his feet and walked across the deck. "What did you do, Jim? Did you have Caryn wrapped in the tarp, just waiting until we dropped anchor that evening so that you could throw her body into the Long Island Sound? Is that what happened? Kate Walter stated that on the night of the party she saw a cabin cruiser and heard a splash. She assumed that the body might have been dropped from the other boat. But the splash she heard was the one you created when you threw Caryn Cooper's body overboard."

McCall tensed, and Jack knew immediately that he had hit another nerve. "Let me tell you what we believe happened. Jump in any time and let us know if we're wrong."

"You weren't happy that Sam Cooper was paying off your loan, but you knew you had no alternative but to accept his help. You also knew that there would be strings attached. That there would be a payment that you couldn't afford. So you called Caryn and asked her to meet you. I'm not sure what you told her that would cause her to leave the house in the early morning hours, but my guess is that gave her the impression that you had to talk to her about something urgent. You were hoping that if you could get her alone, that you would be able to reason with her. That you would be able to convince her to abandon the idea of taking over the *Aphrodite*."

McCall didn't respond, but his hands gripped the railing behind him tightly.

"What did you do when she came on board the boat? Offer her a drink that was drugged? Lull her into a false sense of security?"

"I loved Caryn! I would never hurt her," McCall admitted.

"But she didn't reciprocate your love," Jack said as McCall began to pace along the deck. "She was in love with her husband."

"Sam was no good for her. He was controlling. Jealous," McCall stated harshly, not even aware that he was falling into Jack's trap.

"And that bothered you. You didn't understand how she could have loved someone like that. So you took it upon yourself to try and break them up. Even using your own employees, Joe Cooper and Tim Camp."

"I didn't use them!"

"Yes, you did. You made sure that you fed Tim's interest in Caryn's life with his father, and you led just enough emotional support to Joe to win his trust. You didn't want to take any chances that he would begin to question your feelings for Caryn."

"Caryn would have been better off without Sam!"

"Except she didn't see it that way, so you had to try and change her mind."

McCall shook his head. "Caryn was blind to Sam's faults. She thought the sun rose and set by his command."

Jack waited a few moments to see if McCall would say anything else. When he didn't, Jack pushed his agenda a little further. "And that was the problem. You didn't understand how Caryn could feel so deeply toward Sam. That just didn't make sense to you. And when you found out that it was Caryn who actually wanted to take over control of the *Aphrodite,* you felt betrayed."

"No!"

The quickness of McCall's response told Jack more than words that the man was close to confessing. Jack changed tactics. "Then tell us what happened that night, Jim. Talk to us. If Caryn's death was an accident, say so. We can help you if you let us."

When McCall still hesitated, Jack pressed. "Do you really think that you cleaned up that well? DNA tests are being done on Caryn's clothing as we speak. If she was with you that night, if you touched her, we'll know about it. We have enough of your DNA from the searches done at your home and on board this ship to run the tests. Do you really want to take the chance on the DNA samples coming back clean? More important, can you afford to? After everything you revealed already, you and I both know that there will be a DNA match somewhere. That's all the district attorney needs to take this case to court. Everything you said about your relationship will be brought up. Witnesses that saw you alone together will be subpoenaed to testify. That's a lot of evidence for the jury to consider. Think about it, Jim. Are you willing to let things go that far? Or are you going to talk to us? To explain what happened that night. Explain how everything got so out of control."

McCall's eyes drifted to the railing, and Jack sensed that he was waging an inner battle with himself. Knowing that he could go either way, that he could speak or hold his silence, Jack tried once more to reason with him. "We can help you if you let us."

McCall was silent for long moments before his eyes slowly rose to meet Jack's. "Caryn was here that night. I had left a message on her cell phone telling her that it was important that I speak to her as soon as possible. That it was urgent."

Jack felt the pressure ease. "Did you tell her why?"

"No. I just told her that I would be on board the *Aphrodite* by four A.M. to start preparing the ship for that evening's cruise. I knew she would come in the morning. She was a morning person and frequently got up early to jog. It was one of the things we had in common."

"Why did you ask her to come?"

"I needed to know why Sam wanted controlling interest in the *Aphrodite*."

"And that's when you found out that it wasn't Sam, but rather Caryn who wanted to be a part of the business."

"Yes. When Caryn arrived, she thought something had happened. She was concerned by my message. When she realized I just wanted to talk, she agreed to stay for coffee. We were in the dining salon when she said she was looking forward to being a partner on the boat. The comment stunned me. I didn't expect her to say that. I thought the idea was Sam's." McCall's eyes met Jack's once more. "You were right before. I felt betrayed. I wanted to know how she could do that to me. I honestly thought that we shared something special. I knew she didn't love me, but I thought she at least cared." He became lost in his own thoughts. "Things got heated, and she tried to leave. I just grabbed her arm to pull her back. I wasn't looking to hurt her, but she lost her balance and fell."

"And hit her head on the deck," Jack said, thinking back to the bruise that the medical examiner had uncovered.

"Yes. I tried to wake her up but I couldn't. Her breathing was really shallow, and eventually I couldn't even detect it. I thought she was dead. If I had any idea that she was alive . . ."

"What happened then?"

McCall looked at him with haunted eyes. "I panicked. I didn't know what to do. I laid Caryn in a tarp and wrapped her up in it."

"Effectively suffocating her," Jack said, watching McCall flinch.

"I didn't know," McCall murmured, almost in a whisper.

"Is that when you decided to dispose of the body?"

McCall pushed a restless hand through his hair. "I wasn't thinking clearly. I didn't know what else to do. I had an old anchor on board. One that I had purchased to have mounted on the wall in one of the staterooms. I acted without thinking. I hid the body in the engine compartment until we set sail on the night of Ed Stall's birthday. I waited until we anchored offshore and everybody was involved with the party."

"And then you threw her body overboard."

McCall expelled a breath. "Yes."

Jack looked over at Ryan, who had stood by quietly. With a slight nod, Jack communicated to him that he should get in touch with Ed.

After casting a quick glance at McCall, Ryan left to make the call.

"I honestly never meant to hurt Caryn. I would never have intentionally hurt her," McCall said, almost to himself.

Jack handcuffed McCall and read him his rights.

"I'd like to call my lawyer," McCall said.

"You can call your attorney once we get to the police station." Jack escorted McCall to the dock where Ryan waited.

"Everything okay?" Ryan asked.

Jack nodded. "Did you get in touch with Ed?"

"Yeah. He's sending a team out to the ship now to secure the area, and he'll be waiting at the station. Why don't you take McCall in and I'll stay here until the team arrives. I'll have someone give me a lift later and I'll meet you there."

"All right," Jack said, casting one final look at the gleaming yacht before turning to McCall. "Come on. Let's go."